welcome to your life

KATRINA MARIE

Editor: Small Edits

Cover Design: Y'all that Graphic

To those of you that find yourself in difficult situations.
Don't be deterred, you've got this.

welcome to your life

prologue

THERE'S nothing like sitting around a bonfire in the beginning of summer. It's already hot as Hades, and this whole shindig is ridiculous. I know it's supposed to be our last big party since we graduated a few hours ago, but I'm pretty much over it. It's the same people and the same place. Doesn't anyone get tired of seeing each other all the damn time?

I'm in shorts and a tank top, standing as far away from the monstrosity of flames as I can, and I'm still sweating. I'm surprised the police haven't been called out here by concerned neighbors. The flames are definitely high enough to be seen from town. But I guess being in the middle of a field on private property keeps that from happening. Jake and his buddies didn't plan this well at all. We should be at a pool somewhere, or hell, even the lake. Everyone thought it was a great idea since the star athlete suggested it. I voiced my opinion, but it went unheard.

Jake is standing with a few of his friends as I head

toward him. I don't feel like being here anymore. I'd much rather be home, curled up in bed and reading a book.

"I'm ready to go," I tell Jake when I reach him. He completely ignores me, like he always does when we're at these parties. Don't get me wrong, he's a nice guy, but when he starts drinking he goes into asshole mode.

I tap him on the arm, "I said I'm ready to go, Jake."

He whirls around on me. And I can already tell by that glazed look in his eyes that he's going to be a jerk.

"Well, I'm not. Go hang out with Cami, or something." He glares at me, daring me to argue with him.

"Cami is hooking up with some guy. It's hot, and I'm tired of standing around." I know I should keep my mouth closed, but I don't like being told what to do.

"Too damn bad, Tonya. I'm not leaving, so chill the fuck out." He roars, making sure his point is made.

This statement right here pisses me off more than anything. I don't understand why he thinks he can treat me like shit when he starts drinking. Is it some kind of man code or something? I know some of the other guys don't act like this, but the sad fact is, most of them do.

I stare Jake down, and when he won't give an inch, I unleash. "Who the hell do you think you are? We've been dating a long time, but that does not mean you can talk to me like I'm worthless." I take a deep breath before continuing, "I'm leaving, and I don't care if I have to *walk* all the way home." I shout. "I'm tired of this shit, and can't take it anymore."

I notice everything has gone eerily quiet, and I glance around. Just fucking great. We've attracted a crowd. That was not my intention, but I can't deal with this anymore.

It's the same thing every weekend, and I'm just tired of it. I love Jake, or at least, I want to. It would be so much easier that way. He's the golden boy of our high school and everyone keeps telling me I should be grateful that he picked me. And I was for a long time. But now – now everything just feels strained. Disconnected. We've started drifting apart and most days I feel like I'm just going through the motions. Like we both are. Staying together because it's easier than breaking up. Definitely easier than being alone. Or at least it was, but I'm over being treated like his pretty little lapdog.

I start walking toward the driveway, and come to a halt when I hear him yelling behind me.

"That's okay bitch, keep walking. Now I don't have to deal with your moody ass anymore." He's laughing like he doesn't have a care in the world.

I want to beat the hell out of him so bad. But I don't really want to cause any more of a scene. I already know that I'll be the talk of the town tomorrow, and giving them more fuel to gossip wouldn't be a good idea. I flip Jake the finger and continue on my merry way.

I should probably call my parents to come pick me up, but I'm a little buzzed and don't want to get a lecture. Their little vacation to celebrate my graduation means they aren't home anyway. Walking is probably the dumbest idea I've had today. Well... besides telling Jake off in front of everyone. That ranks right up there at the top.

I come to stop when I know I'm far enough away from the party that nobody will see me, and pull out my phone to call Cami. I'm sure she's already heard about what happened, but I need her just the same. The ringing from the phone sounds loud compared to the still quiet of the night.

Finally, she picks up. "Oh my gosh, what happened? Where are you? Dammit T, answer me."

Even though I'm beyond frustrated I can't help but chuckle. Only she would get worked up into a tizzy without letting me explain anything.

"I'm fine. I'm down the road. Any chance you want to pick me up, and take me home?" I ask.

"Not a problem at all. I'll be there in just a sec."

"Thanks," I breathe, right before hanging up.

Cami is on her way, but I still keep walking. I want to put as much distance between Jake and myself as I can. But just thinking about that asshat has me fuming once again.

Before I can march back to the party and give him a piece of my mind, a car pulls up beside me.

The window comes down, and Cami leans toward it. "Get in, hot stuff."

I smile and slide into the car. Cami looks at me expectantly. I know she wants all the details of what just went down, but I'm not sure if I'm ready to talk about it. I'm still angry and hurt. Finally, she lets off the brake and we make our way down the dusty, dirt road.

As we're pulling up to my driveway, I shift my body and face Cami. She puts the car in park, and stays put. Waiting for me to speak.

"I'm pretty sure I just broke up with Jake." My voice catches, and a tear slides down my face. I hate that I cry when I'm angry. It's one of my many misgivings that really pisses me off.

"Yeah, I heard," Cami replies. "But how he behaved?

That was inexcusable. I didn't catch the part where you went off on him, but I heard the backlash when I was looking for my car to come pick you up."

"Oh great. I can't even imagine what he's telling everyone." I bury my face in my hands, and try to rub this horrible night out of existence.

"Don't even worry about it, girl. You did yourself a favor. Now, stop angry crying. Let's go inside and eat all the chocolate your mom has stashed in the freezer." She lifts my chin until I'm looking at her. She knows I can't resist chocolate.

"That," my voice cracks and I clear my throat. "That sounds like a fantastic idea."

This is definitely a much better way to spend graduation night. With my best friend by my side, and chocolate to eat to ease my troubles.

one

"YOU HAVE GOT to be fucking kidding me," I say under my breath. There's no way this can be happening. I had my whole future ahead of me. What am I supposed to do now? My parents are going to kill me, and I can't rely on my ex-boyfriend, Jake. He's likely to run away, scared shitless.

Goodbye scholarships. I'm only eighteen, and this isn't how I envisioned my life turning out. I wipe the tears from my cheeks. When did I start crying? I grab the little stick that has now determined my future, wrap it in toilet paper, and hurl it in the trash.

Gathering all the strength I can muster, I walk out of the bathroom, gathering the words to tell my parents that they will soon be grandparents. This isn't going to go well at all.

I'm completely overcome with the many emotions swirling through my brain. Fear, sadness, confusion. I can't settle on just one. I feel each one with every fiber of my being.

My parents are on the patio drinking in the summer

night, waiting on the first fireworks to sail into the air as we celebrate our freedom. I definitely don't feel free right now. I feel trapped, and can't breathe. The heat isn't helping, either. They look at me as I step on the patio, and instantly know that something is wrong.

"What happened? Are you okay?" My mom asks.

I can only shake my head, look at the ground, and try to keep the moisture behind my eyes. Dad has a look on his face... A mixture of worry and anger.

"Please, don't tell me what I think you are about to tell me," he says. Barely containing the worry that wants to claw its way out.

The tears that I had strangled only moments ago burst free.

"Damn it, Tonya. What the hell are you going to do now?"

I could handle Mom's wrath, but hearing the disappointment in Dad's outburst rips me wide open.

I've always been Daddy's little girl, his pride and joy. But the moment the words "I'm pregnant" slip through my lips, I know he's never going to look at me the same again.

I can't stop the sobs from overtaking my body. To my shock, Mom wraps her arms around me and murmurs soothing words into my hair. I'm not sure what she tells Dad, but he stomps inside, slamming the door behind him.

She isn't happy about the situation, but she understands there's nothing I can do about it now. I refuse to punish this child for my choices, and I hope I can become the strong mother that I have now. I don't know what I would do without her, and having her support means the world to me.

It went about as well as I expected. I knew there was

going to be yelling, and crying, and slammed doors. I hate disappointing them more than anything. They've always supported everything I've wanted to do. And how do I repay them? By announcing they are going to be grandparents when I have no boyfriend, and no plans to fall back on.

Don't get me wrong, I fully intend on going to college, but I have a feeling it's going to be much harder now. I'll have to figure out where I'm going to work, what kind of class schedule I can handle. And what I'm going to *do* with my life. This is definitely not how I planned on spending my summer.

I finally felt like I had a grip on my life. Things have been hard since I broke up with Jake. Until now, that was one of the most difficult situations I've encountered.

How am I supposed to raise a child on my own? How am I going to explain all of this to Jake? Will he even care?

I need Cami with me, now. I need all of her wise wisdom. I know she'll have my back, even if nobody else does. I can already hear the whispers that will be floating from person to person. I don't really care what they think, but I *despise* being part of the rumor mill. I need to figure out how I'm going to handle everything.

I pull back from Mom's arms, and don't miss the tears streaming down her face.

"I'm sorry, Mom," I say while trying to stop the water flowing down my cheeks.

Mom is wiping the damp smudges off my face. "Sweetheart, you have nothing to apologize for. This isn't something you planned. Things are going to be hard, but your father and I will support you no matter what happens."

I grab her hands, and squeeze her fingertips. "Thank

you. I think I'm going to call Cami and see if she wants to come over. Is that okay?"

"Absolutely," she says. "You do whatever you need to do. I'll go make some brownies, and we can make it a girls' night while we watch the fireworks."

I hug my mom. It's the only way I can express how much I love and appreciate her right now. We don't always get along, but I know she just wants what's best for me.

I leave Mom in the kitchen, and head to my room. Grabbing my phone from the desk, I kick off my flip flops and watch them sail across the room. I guess there was a little more frustration in that kick than I thought.

I pull up Cami's number, and text her.

Me: *I need you to come over ASAP!*
Cami: *Consider me there. I need to escape this nuthouse.*
Me: *Awesome... Mom's making brownies.*
Cami: *I'll be there in 5. You know I love brownies.*

I throw my phone on my bed, grab my headphones and zone out to *Bush* while I wait for Cami to get here.

I don't quite realize how zoned out I am. Cami is clapping her hands right in front of my face. I jump back. "What the hell, woman?"

Cami shrugs. "You didn't answer me when I called your name. I figured getting a little up close and personal would snap you out of your head."

I grab her hand and drag her to the kitchen. As soon as we're seated at the kitchen counter, I turn to look at her. I'm pretty sure she knows something is up. I very rarely send her emergency texts.

"So, there's something I need to tell you," I say while gauging her expression. She's worried. Her eyebrows are slanted, and her mouth is puckered like she just smelled something horrible.

"*Okay*," she drawls out. "What happened? Whose ass do I need to kick?"

"Nobody's," I laugh. Of course this girl goes straight to violence. This is why I love her. She's my sister from another mister, and always has my back.

"I'm not sure how to say this," I stammer. "But there will be another person added to the family in about eight to nine months."

All the worry is gone from her face. "Oh my GOSH, you're going to have a new brother or sister." She turns to my mom. "Congrats, Ma. I bet that was quite a shock."

Mom just shakes her head. Cami turns to me waiting for me to fill her in on the point she so obviously missed.

"No, I'm not going to have a new sibling. I like being an only child, thank you very much. But... I'm going to be a mom."

I don't think I've ever seen Cami speechless. She *always* has something to say. But right now, she's staring at me with her mouth gaping open.

I reach over, and push her bottom jaw up. "You're going to catch flies if you leave your mouth open like that."

She starts shaking her head. "Are you sure? I mean, absolutely positive? Did you tell Jake?"

I give my head a quick shake. "You're the third person

I've told. I broke the news to Mom and Dad before I texted you."

Mom looks over at me and gives me a small, sad smile. She knows this is going to affect me in ways I've yet to imagine.

Cami looks around the kitchen, at a loss of what to say. Finally, she asks, "Are you going to tell Jake?"

I put my head against the cool, marble countertop. "I don't know," I mumble. "I know I should, but a part of me is terrified of how he'll react. You know we didn't end things on great terms, and I'm worried he'll use it as a tactic to get back together. I don't want that."

I feel fingers running through my hair, and a hand patting my back. I turn my head to see Cami looking at me. But I don't see pity on her face. She has her battle face on. The one that lets me know she's going to help me get through life in any way possible. And in that moment, I wish I wasn't an only child. I wish I had Cami as my actual sister. But the love we have for each other is stronger than I imagine any sibling bond could ever be.

The timer on the oven goes off, and I jump up. Mom rushes to get the brownies out of the oven, and sets them on the stove top. Cami is already making her way to the pan, and is about to grab a chunk when Mom slaps her hand. "You have to let it cool down, weirdo. You'll burn the hell out of your hand, and I don't think we need to add a hospital visit on top of today's revelations."

Cami sighs, "I guess. But I would totally be okay with a burnt hand if I got to have some of that." She points toward the pan of brownies.

Mom laughs. "You two go outside. I'll bring you a bowl

with brownies and ice cream. The fireworks are about to start and I don't want to miss them."

Cami and I leave her to do her thing, and climb onto the hammock. We are snuggled up against each other, like we used to do when we were kids. I sigh knowing that soon I won't be able to get into this thing in a few months. Cami senses my sadness, reaches over and grabs my hand letting me know I'm going to get through it. And that she'll be my side.

The sky lights up with color, and we stare in awe. This time next year, there will be a little person with the same look in their eyes. I'm mostly terrified thinking about it, but I'm also a little excited.

two

IT'S BEEN two weeks since Dad has talked to me. I may sound like a lost little girl, but I miss him. He's always been my rock. The one I go to whenever I have a problem and need advice. Him not talking to me is killing me inside. It's bad enough I have all these emotions running rampant through me, but to also lose the support of my father... It makes everything a million times worse.

I'm lying on my bed trying to come to grips with all the ways my life is going to change. And the heartache I'm feeling now really sucks. I've tried talking to Cami about it, but she's not very close to her parents. They pretty much suck in the being supportive department. I've never seen a family ignore how special their children are. I think Cami secretly wishes her dad would stop talking to her the way mine has. It'd probably make her life a little easier.

I'm about to get up when my phone pings with a new text message.

Cami: *Are you up?*

Me: *Yeah... why?*

Cami: *Get dressed. I'm coming to pick you up. You need to get out of the house.*

Me: *Ok. See you in a bit. I'm not sure if Mom and Dad are here, so let yourself in.*

Cami: *Chop chop girlfriend.*

Me: *I'd get ready faster if you weren't texting...*

Cami: *And this is the last one.*

I take a quick shower. I wouldn't put it past my best friend to sneak in here and flush the toilet while I'm in there. I wipe the steam from the mirror, and take a second to look at myself. In a few short months I'll have a baby bump. I won't have the slim figure I have now. I won't be able to wear the clothes I love. Does my hair look healthier? It seems like it has a little extra shine to it.

I place a hand on my lower stomach. What is this going to feel like? I don't know what to expect, and that terrifies me.

I hear my bedroom door slam open, and know Cami is here. She's the only person who just barges in. If you ever want privacy, you're out of luck with her. She has no problem pushing your boundaries, or letting you know what she thinks. The only time that's different is when she's home with her parents. She's almost like a Stepford Wife at her house.

"You better be getting dressed, woman." Cami yells through the bathroom door.

I walk into the bedroom with my bath towel wrapped around me.

She eyes me from head to toe. "That is the opposite of having clothes on."

I know she wants me to speed it up, but I just want to continue my life altering pity party. Cami walks to my closet grabs the first shirt she finds. Then she heads toward my dresser, pulls the middle drawer open, and yanks out a pair of shorts.

"Here, put these on," she orders. "And get your own damn bra and panties. I'm not going through those drawers." Cami turns around and marches right out of my room.

"How do you know if these will even fit me?" I holler, so that she can hear me.

She yells back, "Because your OCD tendencies won't let you keep crap that you don't use."

Okay, so she has a point there. I do tend to get rid of stuff that doesn't fit me, or that I don't wear anymore. I dress as quickly as I can, and put my hair up into a messy bun. I hope she doesn't plan on going anywhere that requires me to be all prettied up.

I leave my room, and head to the living room where I find Cami and Dad talking. He's asking her if she's ready for college. She's nodding her head and telling him how excited she is to get out of Asheville. But I can see the sadness in her eyes. I know there's a story there, but I also know she'll shrug it off and tell me everything is fine. We all know that when a woman says she's "fine" she's upset about something.

"Are you ready Cami?"

I look at my dad, willing him to *look* at me, and see more than the mistakes I made. Is this standoff going to last until the baby gets here? I sure hope not. I don't want to spend the next eight months walking on eggshells.

Cami glances at me. "Yep, ready when you are."

"Let's go, then." I'm still waiting on Dad to acknowledge that I'm even in the room. He looks up... But he looks through me, not at me, and offers a small wave. My heart sinks a little more.

Cami insists on driving, and we're jamming to the soundtrack of our childhood. Justin Timberlake and Britney Spears croon through the speakers. I'm going to miss days like this when she's away at college.

I'm shocked when we pull up to the mall thirty minutes later, though I shouldn't be. If there's anything Cami loves more than hanging out with her friends, it's shopping. I keep telling her she should look at careers in design, but she always has some excuse about it being just a hobby.

"Why are we here? It's Saturday, do you know how freaking crowded this place is going to be?"

She glares at me. "This is why I told you to hurry the hell up. It's not my fault you didn't listen. And we're here to start shopping for your maternity wardrobe."

"But why? I'm not anywhere close to showing yet. My damn clothes still fit, stop trying to rush my body getting huge. And what if someone sees us shopping in the maternity store? I haven't told anyone outside of the family that I'm pregnant." I ramble.

She sighs. "Another reason I wanted to get here early. Most of the idiots we went to high school with won't be rolling out of bed for a few hours. So I think we're good. And I won't be here to help you pick out adorable, yet functional maternity clothes. If I leave it up to you, you'll be walking around in sweatpants and ratty t-shirts."

She knows me way too freaking well. "Okay, we'll hit the maternity store first. We'll just have to stop somewhere and buy something so we can put whatever I buy into a different bag. And then... Food. I'm starving."

I'm so happy Cami thought to do this with me. Seriously, she thinks of everything. I'd be completely lost without her. I don't even know what most of this stuff is, but Cami is making sure I get only cute clothes. Nothing that will make me look frumpy.

It's still a little early as we leave the store. I doubt anyone we know will be out and about just yet.

"Let's get some food really quick. I don't think I can let myself go hungry any longer." I say while leading Cami toward the food court.

"I thought you wanted to stop at another store so we can hide the evidence," she says bewildered.

"What's the likelihood that we're going to see someone we know? It's barely eleven thirty. I think we're good."

We order pretzels. I don't want anything super heavy, and I want to savor these moments I have with my best friend.

I'm in the middle of taking a bite of my pretzel when Cami's eyes widen. Whatever has that look on her face can't be good. I turn around and see Jake standing behind me... and he's staring at the bag with the huge maternity logo on it.

I guess I don't have much of a choice anymore. He's going to find out *now*.

three

THIS IS NOT how I pictured this conversation going down. I was hoping to have a little more time to figure out if I even wanted to tell Jake. But that has clearly been taken out of my hands.

"What is that?" He asks uncertainly.

I peer up at him while he looms over me with a scowl that would make any other girl weep. "It looks like a shopping bag, Jake."

"I can see that, *Tonya*. But why is it from that maternity store?" He asks.

I sigh, and my shoulders sag because we are definitely doing this now. "It's from the maternity store because I'm pregnant... And you're going to be a daddy."

I can see every single emotion he has work it's away across his face. Some of them are the same ones I felt not too long ago, and still feel now. What I don't expect is that last look on his face. He's smirking, and has a gleam in his eye that tells me I'm not going to like what he has to say next.

"Then I guess that means we should get back together. I

need to do right by you and this baby." He says it like I didn't just give him life changing news.

"N-n-no," I stammer. "That is definitely not what that means. I honestly wasn't even going to tell you about me being pregnant."

Jake's brows furrow, and from the frown curving his mouth, he didn't expect me to say that. He pulls out a chair to sit next to me, and I jump up from my seat. I get Cami's attention and bob my head toward the exit. I'm not about to hash this out here, in the mall. Things could get ugly, and all we need is a bunch of people butting into our business.

"Sorry, Jake. Gotta run." I say as I speed walk my way toward the other side of the mall.

Cami jogs to catch up. I peek behind me, and see Jake still sitting at the table staring at us as we make our departure.

Once we get to the car I feel like I can finally breathe again. Cami slides into the driver seat, and faces me. She has one eyebrow arched, and she's waiting on me to explain myself.

I shrug. "That could have gone a bit better."

Cami bursts out laughing. "You can say that again. I honestly didn't think anyone we knew would be there so early. So are you going to call him later, or at least explain some things?"

"I don't know," I mutter, defeated. "I know I need to, but as you can see he's already hoping we will get back together. And I just... can't."

Cami starts the car, turns on the radio, and starts singing whatever pop song is "hot" right now. I sit back and think about what I'm going to tell Jake and how everything went wrong between us.

We used to be great together. We were a couple for two years. We had all those puppy love feelings. I used to get warm fuzzies around him. He'd bring me flowers out of his mom's garden, and say all the right things. We were the *golden couple* that everyone envied. But as time went on, things started to change.

We started going to all the parties that I never wanted to be at. He would drink and turn into a jerk. At first, he never directed his shitty attitude toward me. But then he started belittling me in front of all his friends. Cami was awesome and would stand up for me, but I would constantly make excuses for him. He was drinking and he didn't mean anything. I finally had my fill the night of graduation.

He said things were going to change. That he was going to try harder to be a better boyfriend. He made prom night romantic and I felt all the feelings that I had felt in the beginning. And that lasted a whole freaking month before asshole Jake made his reappearance.

And then it hits me... I'm a fucking statistic. You hear those stories about girls that get pregnant on prom night, and think it could never happen to you. But it did happen to me. This is going to change the course of my life, and I'm not going to let Jake drag me back down that road again.

Cami snaps her fingers in front of my face. I've zoned out and don't even realize we are back at my house.

"How long have we been here," I ask.

"Oh, about five minutes," Cami replies. "You looked pretty deep in thought, and I didn't want to interrupt that. But it's ridiculously hot, and I want to go inside. And then, you're going to tell me what gave you that huge frown your sporting right now."

"You aren't going to let me out of this, are you?"

She grins. "Absolutely not. We have to figure out how you're going to handle the whole Jake situation, and I have a feeling that look on your face has something to do with him."

I can't help it, I laugh. "You'd be correct."

We walk inside and head straight for my room. After throwing our bags on the bed we change into comfortable clothes, or as the rest of the world knows them as, yoga pants and a tank top.

Now that we're back at home, I don't know what to do.

"So what do you want to do?" I ask Cami.

"Well, I'm going to pull up *Buffy* on Netflix, and you're going to tell me what had you so zoned out back there."

I groan. "I was just trying to figure out how the hell I got here."

Cami is about to make some smart-ass comment. I can feel it coming.

"And before you say anything, I know how we got home. I mean, how did I get to this point in my life? Things with Jake were great for a while until he went all 'I man, you woman. You do what I say.'"

Cue eye roll from Cami. I know her better than she knows herself sometimes.

"You better not be considering getting back with him just because he's your baby daddy," Cami scolds.

"I told you before... That's *not* happening." I start cackling because I've just realized, I do in fact, have a "baby daddy" now.

"I know that's what you said," Cami proclaims. "But that doesn't mean you aren't going to change your mind when he tries to charm his way back into your life. You're better off without him."

"Can we not do this right now?" I ask. "I have to figure out what my next step is. He obviously knows, but I don't know what to do now."

Cami shrugs. "Your mom would probably know how to handle this situation. She deals with impossible people every day selling houses."

"This is why I love you," I say as I throw my hands around her. "You always have the best ideas, even though I should have come up with that one first."

Let the *Buffy* marathon begin. I could use an ass-kicking muse to get me ready for the upcoming confrontation with Jake.

four

IT'S BEEN ALMOST a month and I still haven't heard from Jake. I'm shocked. I figured he'd be pounding on my door the same day he saw us at the mall. I hid in my room for that day feigning illness hoping Mom would send him on his way. But that obviously didn't happen.

This showdown needs to happen soon. He leaves for college soon, and I want this whole thing put behind me before he does. If push comes to shove, I'll go to him. It's not what I want to do. I'd rather have the awaiting conversation on my turf, but it needs to be done.

I'm in the kitchen helping Mom clean up after breakfast, her Saturday morning ritual, when the doorbell rings. I jump. I'm not expecting anyone, and Cami usually uses her key to come in. A feeling of dread fills the pit of my stomach. Looks like I'm getting my wish.

I tiptoe to the window by the door and take a quick peek. Yep, Jake is standing there. Now I'm kind of wishing he wasn't. I know, I know. I need to get it over with, but like

Cami said before... Can I resist his charm and stand my ground?

I slowly open the door and lean against the frame. "Hi Jake."

He looks down and shuffles his feet. "Are you going to invite me in?"

"That depends. Are you going to try to talk me into getting back with you? If so, you can turn around, get in your car and leave," I say. Yay me for sounding more confident than I feel.

"I can't promise that... But I'll do my best to hear what you have to say, and I hope you do the same," he says. Finally looking at me. I can tell he's serious because he's actually looking into my eyes. Something he usually never does.

"Okay, then I guess you can come in," I say, opening the door wider and stepping to the side.

Jake walks to the couch and plops down. I listen for sounds coming from the kitchen, but I guess Mom figured we needed a little bit of privacy. I'm happy she has that much faith in my decisions, but I also wish she was sitting at the table listening in. That way she can come save me if I need it.

I take a seat in the plush recliner adjacent to the couch. It's more comfortable than the couch, but I also don't want too sit to close to him right now.

"So, do you want to start, or do you want me to?" I ask and pull the blanket off the back of the recliner so that I have something to keep my hands busy.

"How long did you know you were pregnant before I saw

27

you at the mall?" He gazes at me with hurt filling his brown eyes.

"Just a couple of weeks."

"Why didn't you tell me sooner? I would have been here for you."

I sigh. "Because I had to figure out my emotions about it all, and I'm still struggling with that. Why did it take you so long to come talk to me?"

He looks down at his clenched hands. "I needed to get myself under control. I was so fucking angry with you for not telling me. And then I realized that I handled the situation badly that day. I do still want to get back together. That's not going to change."

I'm playing with the fringe on the blanket trying to get the words in my head ordered the right way. "That's not going to happen. We broke up because we weren't right for each other anymore. Our love for each other wasn't enough anymore. You'll always have a place in my heart, but this baby isn't enough for me to jump back into your arms."

Jake frowns. He's eyebrows angry slants set on his face. "Why not? Being with you and our baby is the right thing to do. Do you know what people are going to say about you? About me?"

Now I'm getting pissed. "So that's why you want to do this? So the star athlete doesn't look like a complete fuck up?" I take a deep breath. "I don't want to be with you and damn sure not for appearances. Do you realize how much of an ass you sound like right now?"

Jake's shoulders slump. "Were you even going to tell me?"

"Yes... No... Eventually. I've been in shock for the past month. And I knew you would try to use the pregnancy as a bargaining chip. As angry as I am with you right now for that, I also don't want you to ruin your future. You have a full scholarship to play a sport that you love. You can't give that up. Besides, I'm perfectly capable of raising a child. I also have my parents for support and help. I'd like that from you too."

Jake starts to interrupt, but I hold my finger up. "But not as anything more than the father of our child, and maybe a friend."

He shakes his head. "I can't do that. I can't watch you raise our child without being here for you as your other half." He stands up with so much force the sofa scoots back a bit. "I need to go, but know that this isn't over. I will do everything in my power to make things right with us. This kid needs a whole family."

Before I can say anything else, Jake storms toward the door. He gives me one last look before opening it and walking out.

This hurts a lot more than it should. I pull the blanket over my head. The sun shining through the window makes it stifling under here, but I need to hide away from the world for a while. I know Mom will come in here soon to see how everything is going, and I don't want her to see the tears streaming down my face. I don't even know why I'm crying. I should be happy I didn't give in to him, but I know this is a chapter closing.

I was hoping he would be relieved that I didn't want to put the burden of a child on him, but he's definitely angry. I don't know if he wants to get back with me because he actually cares, or to save face in this small town. I can't worry about that right now though. I need to focus on what's ahead. Jake is my past, and this little baby bean is my future.

five

I CAN'T BELIEVE I'll be starting my freshman year of college on Monday. Well, more like almost finished with my freshman year. Thanks to Mom making me take dual credit classes in high school, I already have a couple of my English and History credits out of the way. The only thing I'll need to repeat is Calculus. I honestly don't see why I need that stupid math class. There's no way in hell I'm going to use that information in my day to day life.

Earlier this week Mom and I sat down to figure out what classes to take. Luckily, they are still going to help with my college expenses. Even though Dad said they weren't. His exact words, "You decided you were grown up enough to have sex and get pregnant, then you're grown up enough to pay for your education." Mom quickly came to my defense on that fight.

Mom is going to adjust my work schedule around school. I'm going to be taking late afternoon classes Monday through Thursday, an art class on Saturday, and an online class as well. We picked English for that one. I figure it would be the easiest one to tackle online. I mean, it's words... How hard could it actually be. I can't believe I'm giving up my precious Saturday sleep to go to class, but I guess I should get used to the early mornings.

It's the last weekend Cami will be home before her dad takes her off to school, and we're having a slumber party the entire time. She'll be here from Friday until Sunday morning. Mom has loaded up on all the junk food a pair of teenage girls could want.

We are on another binge session of *Veronica Mars* when Cami turns to me with a look of fear in her eyes. "I don't think I want to go to college. I know it's what my parents want, and that I'll probably do great... but what if I don't. And it's going to be hard when we aren't close to each other. Why did I have to choose a college that's taking me so far away from you?"

"You'll do fine," I say. I know she will. She's one of the strongest people I know. You have to be to deal with her parents.

She seems to take my words easily. She doesn't say anything else, and we resume our marathon. After that we curl up in bed, and whisper about all the things she'll miss while she's away. Her dad is strongly encouraging her to get a degree in accounting so he can groom her to take over his accounting firm. I know that's not what she wants to do, but Cami will do it. She doesn't want to deal with the repercussions if she changed *the plan*.

Sunday morning, Cami's dad is there at the ass crack of dawn to pick her up. She doesn't want to leave, but knows she has to.

Teary-eyed she pulls me into a massive bear hug. "I'm

going to miss you so freaking much. I won't be here to oversee the growth of my little niece or nephew. Can't I just stay and go to the community college, too?"

I laugh. "No goofball. You have to go off to school so you can take over the world one business at a time. Little Bean and I will be just fine. Besides, we can talk on the phone or video chat anytime you need me. You're going to do great."

Before she has the chance to say anything, her father is honking his horn. Her signal that she better get in the car now.

I watch them back out of the driveway, tears threatening to spill. I put on a tough facade for her, but I already miss my best friend being by my side. How am I going to get through the next few months without her?

Cami is off to start on the life her father has mapped out for her, and I get things ready for my first week of community college. This is going to be a challenge, but one I will take down with a smile on my face. *I can do this.*

I feel an arm wrap around my shoulders as I watch Cami drive away. I glance up and see my dad looking down at me with a sad smile on his face. "You'll get through it sweetheart. I know I haven't been the easiest to deal with the past few weeks, but I'm always here to help you. With anything you need."

I smile, and throw both arms around my father's waist. He isn't much on emotional talks, but that small gesture lets me know that everything will be okay.

* * *

The first week of classes went pretty well. Juggling work at the real estate office my mom owns and school hasn't been too bad. But this week is mostly going over the syllabus and rules for each class. Basically... be there, turn in your shit, and you'll likely do well.

I have to get up ridiculously early for my Saturday morning class, and I'm having a hard time falling asleep. I haven't heard from Jake since our argument and that worries me. He's not one to let something go, especially when it's something he wants. So I'm a little bit surprised by the radio silence.

I'm also starting to really freak out. What if I can't do this by myself? I mean this week was easy, of course, but it's going to get harder the further I continue into my college career. Can I really do this? Am I doing my child a disservice by trying to go it alone?

Ugh, I really wish my brain would shut off so I can get some sleep before my class. I don't want to go to class looking and feeling like a zombie. Luckily, I don't seem to be suffering from the dreaded morning sickness that Mom said I would. I'm counting my lucky stars. Work and school would be so much harder if I had to contend with that as well.

Hoping music will soothe my brain, I grab my earbuds and put them in my ears. I go through my music library until I find *Band of Skulls*. The haunting melodies and lyrics do what I intended it to. The song "Bruises" plays as I slowly drift to sleep.

I wake up to my alarm blaring through my earbuds. I'm not sure how long it was going off before it jolted me out of sleep. It's almost eight thirty and my class starts at nine. I jump out of bed, brush my teeth, and throw on a pair of shorts and a tank top. It's the first clean thing I see. I guess I'm doing the messy bun thing today. I don't have time to fix my hair or makeup.

I grab a brownie out of the pan Mom has on the counter. Chocolate for breakfast... hell yeah. I yank my keys from the hook by the door, rush to the Jeep, and haul ass out of the driveway. I've got fifteen minutes to make it to class. I don't want to make a bad impression by being late on my first day of this class.

I make it with a few seconds to spare. The professor closes the door right after I walk in. I've got to make sure I set like 5 alarms to get me out of bed on the weekends so this doesn't become a habit.

I find a seat, pull out my notebook, and get ready to start this journey in Art. It's not something I'm particularly interested in, but it's a required course. This class seems like it's going to breeze. Maybe this whole work and college thing won't be so hard.

six

IT'S SATURDAY MORNING, and the last weekend of November. I'm walking, or waddling however you want to look at it, into my art appreciation class. I will never understand why this class is one of the requirements to get a degree. Unless I'm going into that field when I graduate, I don't see the point. This class is usually a snooze fest. We typically watch movies and hand in worksheets about the lame videos we just watched. With the modern world you would think they would update the crap they show us in these classes.

Why did I think I could do this whole single parent thing while going to college? This kid isn't even here yet, and I'm ready to pull my hair out. My mom keeps reassuring me it's pregnancy brain. I don't know if I completely believe that, but it makes sense. Besides the decision that got me into this predicament, I can't seem to think like a sane person anymore.

Everything was going fine the first couple of months, but it seems like lately this pregnancy is wearing me down.

I think I may have taken on too big of a class load. I've gotten grumpier and just moody in general. One minute I'm happy go lucky, and the next I'm like the spawn of Satan. I don't like the way my hormones are all over the place.

Thank goodness finals are a few weeks away. I could definitely use the time to relax and maybe get some reading done. From what everyone has told me, all my favorite things to do will cease to exist once the baby is here. It's hard knowing all of my friends are at big universities having the time of their lives, and I'm at the local college because I can't afford the tuition at a larger school. And the fact that I'm a walking statistic.

My parents have made the longing for the life I could've had easier. They've been extremely supportive despite the initial shock and anger when I first told them the news. That was probably the hardest thing I've ever had to do.

The professor handing out papers snaps me out of my thoughts. This is something that happens every time we freaking meet, but this time they aren't worksheets. After all the papers are out, and we are looking at it like it might grow legs, he clears his throat to get our attention. "Okay guys, I know you are used to getting the continuous worksheets, and don't think I don't realize that most of you are sleeping during the videos. But with finals coming up, I wanted to see what y'all have actually retained from this class. I want you to pick an artist, your favorite one, and recreate one of their works. It can be any artist from any era. I will only allow one student per artist. They are so many out there that I don't think this will be a problem. So, instead of boring you with any more videos this time, we are going to the computer lab so that you can search for your subject piece."

Hands are already being raised with students wanting to pick some of the more well-known artists but Professor Thompson shuts that down immediately. "I'm not taking your requests right now. You'll research for forty-five minutes, and then you can come see about approval for the work you'll be recreating."

We head to the computer lab, Professor Thompson trailing behind us. I already know I want to do a Picasso piece. I'm sure there are others, but I plan on being the one that seeks out the professor first. I don't know when I became infatuated with Picasso's work. I think it was in my history class in high school. We were learning about different wars and battles in different countries. One day we started reading about the battle at Guernica. I didn't think much of it until I saw a painting that Picasso did about the battle. There was so much despair and destruction, but the piece was beautiful. The colors were muted, all black and shades of gray. I could feel the heartache of this small town. I knew I didn't want to use that piece for my creation, it's too depressing and a little dark. I need something different right now.

I log into the computer and begin searching for all the works available from Picasso. There are so many, some of them I have never seen. Scrolling through the images, one caught my eye. It's called "The Girl in the Mirror." It's not all sunshine and rainbows that's for sure, but something in it calls to me. There are so many emotions and so much depth behind the eyes of the subject of this painting. I know right then that I am going to paint this piece. I stare at the clock waiting for the forty-five minutes to be up. I have to get to Thompson before one of the other students snatches my artist away from me.

I hear a chair begin to roll out from one of the rows behind me. Luckily I picked a spot in the first row and fairly close to where Professor Thompson sits. I bolt out of my chair speed walking, as funny a sight as that is, toward him barely getting there before the person that was coming to give him their choice. Before Thompson can even get his register out to put down my choice I blurt out Picasso. He rolls his eyes prepared to turn me down since he's a well-known artist. I stand my ground. "I'm doing Picasso's "Girl in the Mirror." He looks like he's about to argue, but decides he doesn't want to piss off the obviously emotional pregnant girl before him.

I hear the person behind me growl in frustration. I turn around, ready to lay into them, but forget how to speak. Behind me is a guy with light brown hair that looks like it needs a trim, evidenced by small curls starting to turn upward. He has a cap on to try to tame them. He has the lightest hazel eyes with specs of green throughout them. He's about a head taller than me, and looks pretty pissed off that I picked his artist. But I can't stop staring. How did I go almost an entire semester not knowing this fine specimen of man was in my class?

"Professor Thompson, I was going to pick Picasso."

"Now Reaf, Tonya here has already chosen Picasso. She got here first so you'll need to pick another artist." Professor Thompson adjusts his glasses while noting my artist on his spreadsheet.

Reaf sputters, "But... Why can't we have two people do

the same artist. Many of these works have vast differences, and different looks."

Professor Thompson seems to consider this a moment. He relents, "I guess I can bend the rules a little. Which piece are you wanting to produce?"

Reaf doesn't hesitate, "Guernica."

I stand frozen. How in the hell did I manage to be in the class with someone as gorgeous as him, and who also has the same interest in artwork that I have. Thompson nods his head, "Okay, I'll put you down for that work. Since y'all decided to do the same artist, I want a report from you that shows the diversity in an artist's portfolio... together."

We stand there gaping at him, realizing he's not going to change his mind. Neither one of us is willing to forego the painting we've requested so we agree. I quickly grab my things and head out of the lab prepared to head home.

Someone grabs my arm before I make it very far down the hallway. I turn to see Reaf glaring at me. I guess he thought I would bow out of my choice. Well, tough shit. "I guess since we're working together I'll be seeing more of you."

He takes me in from head to toe, nods, and walks away. Um, okay. I'm not sure what that look was about, but it seems like he just sized me up, and decided I'm some worthless, teenage, pregnant chick. Well, screw him. He has no right to judge me. I pick up my pace to get to my car. It's cold outside, and I really don't want to freeze my ass off before I get home.

seven

MOM IS in the kitchen getting things ready to make dinner when I walk through the door. I can smell cumin, pepper and tomato sauce in the air. I really hope this means she's making my favorite. It would definitely make my crappy day a million times better. Chicken and rice has a way of doing that. It reminds me of my great-grandmother's house, and the love I've always felt around her kitchen.

As I enter the kitchen, Mom asks, "Are you going to be home for dinner?"

I stare blankly at her. Does she not realize that my days of going out are over? "Yeeeahhh," I draw out, making sure she catches that I think her question is absurd. "It's not like I'm a huge party animal nowadays. Besides, I just got my final assignment from Professor Thompson, and I need to see what materials I'll need to pick up after work tomorrow."

Mom gives me that patronizing glare that moms do oh so well. "I was just asking. You know it's not healthy for you to shut yourself in so much. Yes, you are pregnant, but you

41

still have to live. You can't let the world just pass you by because of a bump in the road."

So, this was her ploy. Get me to feel bad because I don't go out. "Well mom, it's not like I have many friends. They are all off on their own adventures. I doubt anyone my age would want to hang out with a pregnant girl. There's a limited amount of trouble I can get into with people. Then they feel all awkward because they pity me."

"I was just trying to help," Mom said.

"I know, but just let me deal with my own feelings. They are already out of whack as it is."

Grabbing my bag I head for my room. It's right past the nursery my parents started putting together. They've been gracious enough to let me live with them, but I was shocked when they insisted on making a nursery for the baby bean. Mom keeps getting frustrated with me because I won't open the envelope that has the sex of the child growing inside me. If I open it, and find out what I'm having it will make the situation feel more real than it already does. It's an argument we've gotten in many times. She doesn't know what colors to fill the nursery with. She sees so many adorable baby things but can't buy them because she doesn't know which gender to buy for. I think she's more excited about this kid than I am. After her blow up about my decision not to find out at the doctor's office, I found her snooping through my desk to get the envelope. I had to find a new hiding place for it.

I'm curled up on my bed with that same envelope, running my fingers along the flap. I know I should open it but I can't bring myself to do it. It'll just wait until I'm a little more adjusted to the thought of becoming a mom. You would think it would have hit it by now, but it's just so hard to see myself as a mom. I'm still so young.

Starting up my laptop I pull out some paper so that I can begin making my list of supplies for the art project. I pull up the image of "Girl in the Mirror" and begin writing down the various colors of paints I'll need. I haven't painted much except for what was required of us in our art classes in high school. I decide I'll get two canvases in case I royally screw up at my first attempt. I put the list aside so that it's where I can find it when I head out tomorrow. Mom will have dinner ready soon, and I'm not ready to go down and face her in case she has anything more to say about my choices to not go hang out with so-called friends. I decide to start on this ridiculous report that Thompson is forcing on myself and Reaf. Right now Google is my best friend. I don't feel like going to a library now, it doesn't help that the small Asheville library isn't open today, and I'm not sure how I'm going to do this project with Reaf. He seems like such an arrogant asshole. And he didn't give me any way to contact him to work on this damn thing. This is going to be impossible. I should have just picked a different stupid artist.

I put in my favorite My Little Pony earbuds—yes I'm still a kid at heart—start my playlist and begin my search. There are so many things about Picasso that I didn't know. And for some reason I didn't realize that he's a much more modern artist than I thought. He has always been referenced in art books for as long as I can remember so I always thought he was some classic guy that has been gone for centuries. Shows how much I know about the artist that inspired me so much. His work really does have so many aspects. Many of them are two-sided. They can be dark and beautiful, haunting and magical. I guess that's why I feel this pull toward "Girl in the Mirror." The girl is a thing of beauty, well as beautiful as Cubism allows, but looking at herself in the mirror she sees this ugly, broken girl. It pretty much signifies everything I feel about myself now. I had so much promise, and now... Well now I don't know what I am, or how I feel about myself.

As I jot down notes, I glance at my phone and see the icon blinking signifying I have a message. There isn't anyone that I can think of that would be texting me. I've pretty much written off my social life since finding out that I was pregnant. Curiosity getting the best of me, I grab it and see who is all of a sudden interested in checking in on me. It's from a number I don't know.

Unknown Number: *Meet me tomorrow at 5.*

Um, I don't think so. Random numbers telling me to meet them has got to be some sort of prank, or possibly a serial killer. The fact that my mind jumps to serial killer shows how morbid this whole pregnancy brain thing has made me.

Me: *who is this?*

Less than ten seconds later I get a reply... *Reaf.*

eight

HOW IN THE hell did this guy get my number?

As far as I know, he doesn't know any of the people I used to hang out with. I don't think he even went to my high school. He must have some voodoo mind magic, or he's a stalker. Again with the morbidity there. But seriously, the probability of him being a stalker makes more sense. He just has this mysterious bad boy vibe. He carries himself like he doesn't have a care in the world, and doesn't mind breaking a few rules. It makes me wonder which rules he's likely broken.

Apparently, I've been thinking on this too long. My cell vibrates in my hands, scaring the piss out of me. I jump, and nearly fall out of my chair.

Reaf: *Hello..... are you there?*

Damn, he's freaking impatient. But I look at the last text I received, and realize it's been twenty minutes since he responded.

Me: *Um, okay. Yeah, where at?*

Reaf: *You like coffee? ~R*

Me: *I do like coffee, but in case you haven't noticed I'm not exactly in the position to be able to consume it.*

Reaf: *So, maybe ice cream. I can bring pickles. haha*

So this guy thinks he's a fucking comedian. That right there irritates me more than how he got my phone number. I understand wanting to get this horrible assignment that's been forced on us done, but that doesn't mean he can try to be all annoyingly cute. Wait, what the hell... Did I just refer to dark and gloomy as cute? I'm just going to chalk that up to pregnancy hormones. I definitely don't need to be thinking this guy is any kind of attractive. That's how I got in this mess in the first place.

Me: *Coffee is fine. Smart ass. I'll meet you at Brews Clues at 5.*

And because I'm feeling a little bitchy I add, *Deuces.*

Hopefully he gets the hint to leave me alone. I don't want witty banter with this guy. I just want to get this paper done, turn it in, and get on with my semester break. With all my big plans of lazing about on the couch and binge watching *Buffy* on Netflix for what seems like the millionth time. Oh, and stuffing my face. Because honestly, that's the best part of having a bun in the oven. I can eat whatever I want, and not feel bad about it at all. I hear mom yell down the hall that dinner is ready, so I close the laptop and waddle my way toward the kitchen.

Dad is sitting at the table, which is a huge shocker. He's made himself conveniently absent for most dinners claiming he has meetings with so-and-so, or the CEO. Whatever keeps him from home as often as possible. Don't get me wrong he's been supportive, but he's still not thrilled about the situation I've gotten myself into. Luckily I've been busy with school and work, and when I get home I'm so exhausted that I usually collapse onto my bed. So we haven't exactly been in the presence of the other for too long. I'm not sure how that's going to work out when I don't have school for a month. I'll definitely be home a lot more.

"Hey, sweetie. How was your day at school?" Dad asks.

"It was okay. We got our assignment for our final. And because I wouldn't back down from an artist I chose, I was paired up with a total douchebag to do a joint paper over Picasso."

He fixes me with a stern stare, and I know it's because of the word "douchebag." Dad has never been a fan of my choice in language, and gets all uptight whenever I use crude words. But I think in this instance it totally fits. As far as I can tell Reaf is a total d-bag, you know first impressions and all.

"So, about this final project?" Mom tries to steer the conversation back to a topic that is less likely to get my dad in a tizzy.

"Well, we had to pick a work of art by an artist and we have to recreate it. I picked a piece by Picasso. It has a lot of detail but I think I can manage it between work and my other classes. Most of those are winding down with it being the end of the semester."

They are looking at me like I'm crazy. I know it's because I'm being so animated about the assignment. For once I feel excited about something rather than just going through the daily routine.

Dad chooses this moment to bring the focus back around to the mundane paper that I have to write. "So what about this report you have to do?" He sure knows how to dampen my sudden excitement.

I sigh, "This guuuuy," I draw out the word so that dad knows just how much it pains me not to be completely awful about Reaf, "wanted to do a piece by Picasso also. Thompson must have realized, or known, that neither of us were going to back down, so he told us we had to write a paper about the many areas one artist can cover in their works."

For some reason my dad smiles. He doesn't seem to realize how crappy this whole ordeal is going to be. I've become a recluse since August, and I don't really want to remedy that now. "This will be good for you. You need to hang out with other people your age. You don't want to shut yourself off to the outside world completely." He knows that's exactly what I want to do. I'm not seeing this conversation getting any better, or going in my favor, for that matter so I yawn dramatically. Lucky for me, my parents actually think I'm as sleepy as I sound. Mom nudges my shoulder. "Go ahead and head on to bed. I'll clean up in here."

I scoot my chair back and slide out. Giving mom and dad quick peck on the head I turn and start toward my room. After changing into my footies, it's ridiculously cold and my bed is by the window, I climb into bed with a copy of *Breaking Dawn*. Judge me all you want, it's the best book in the series. I must have been more tired than I thought. I drift to sleep with dreams of vampires and werewolves and promises of unrequited love.

nine

IT'S ENTIRELY TOO EARLY in the morning when I slam my hand on the alarm. I think I've listened to that annoying thing go off for an hour. I do not want to go to work. I know it's Sunday, and I don't really have to, but there are things I need to get done before this next week. Most of the classes I'm in are just doing a review, but I want to devote as much time as possible to this art piece. I feel like doing this project will help me get some of my pent up feelings out. I don't think anyone would understand it if I tried to tell them, but maybe they'll see it in my painting.

Since I'm not trying to impress anyone, especially Reaf, I find my most comfortable pair of yoga pants, a long sleeve T-shirt that shows my Harry Potter love, and a Grouplove hoodie I bought at a concert. I jump in the shower, since I fell asleep last night before taking one. Even if I had taken a shower last night, I would have taken another one. Nothing wakes me up like the spray of hot water first thing in the morning. I rush through my shower, not bothering to wash my hair since I got up late, and throw my clothes on. I put my hair up in a messy bun. It's the best way to hide a missed shampoo. I grab my comfy furry boots and head toward the living room.

Mom is already in the kitchen making coffee. I'm not sure how I came from that woman. She lives for the mornings, and I loathe them with a vengeance. "Morning, Tonya! Do you want me to make you some breakfast?"

I shake my head at her. "No, Mom. I'm already running late. I'll just grab some donuts on the way."

She looks at me exasperated. "You know you don't have to be in at a certain time, much less go in on a Sunday. It's not like your boss is going to get mad at you." With that, she gives me an exaggerated wink. She loves the whole boss joke, seeing as she is my boss.

While I put on my boots I say, "I know mom, but I have to run to the craft store, and then I have to meet Reaf to start on this paper." When I turn her way she's grinning like a crazy person. She seems way too excited about this even though she was trying to show otherwise at dinner last night. "Don't get any ideas, mom. This isn't a date. We are only working on this paper, and I hope not to see him after that." Mom shakes her head, but still has a gleam in her eye like she knows something I don't.

I give her a hug, grab my bag and head out the door. I wish I would've remembered to let the Jeep warm up while I was getting ready. I hate the cold, and it's pretty damn frigid. The Jeep has seen better days. I've had it since I got my license, and it's been very dependable. Let's hope things stay that way for a while. I definitely don't need anything to break down on me now. The heat is blowing full blast, and I wish it would hurry up and get hot in here. I figure while I'm waiting I might as well add some tunes. I plug in my phone, scroll through my music library, and press play when I get to *Walk the Moon*. I know I said I'm not a morning person, but it's hard not to be happy when "Shut Up and Dance" starts blaring through the speakers.

I feel the beginning flickers of warmth blow across my cheeks, and decide it's time to hit the road. Mom's office is only fifteen minutes away, on the other side of town. I make my way to the donut shop and get a pig in the blanket and donut holes. This is how I start my daily food intake way more than I should. But it's just so good, and the food is still warm. I'm stuffing my face as I pull into the parking lot. It's empty because nobody in their right mind gets up this early on the weekend to go to work when they don't have to. I know if I skip today the things Mom needs filed and the contracts she needs pulled will have her running around tomorrow while I'm in class. I don't want to get frantic texts from her while I'm in class and this is the easiest way to avoid that.

I'm putting the last file in the cabinet five hours later. I can't believe the time went by so fast, but I haven't been here a few days and the work piled up. It's like it would kill any of her other assistants to do something, like their job, while I'm at school. They constantly give me shit because I'm working there, and they see it as a hand out. Whatever, they can judge me all they want. It's not the first time people have thought the worst about me. It's two, and I haven't had any lunch. I can almost feel my stomach moving in protest, or maybe that's just the baby. I lock up, get in my car, and head toward the closest burger place.

I can feel everyone staring as I walk in. I've known these

people my entire life, but they treat me like a leper. I guess they're scared they're going to catch the pregnancy by simply breathing the same air as me. I'm probably the example for some of the parents to their daughters, a cautionary tale if you will. I've never understood why the pregnant girl gets all the flack, but the guy doesn't get shit. They are sympathetic toward the male. It's crap, and I have to force myself to keep walking and not pay them any mind.

I'm placing my order, a cheeseburger with extra pickles and fries, when the air behind me shifts. I know who it is without even turning around. How can one interaction, well two interactions, with this guy already have me feeling him when he's around? Best not to think about that little fact too much. I pay for my food, and turn around. Reaf is standing behind me with a smirk curving his mouth. I must stare at his lips a little too long because he clears his throat.

I glance up at him. "Are you stalking me?"

He doesn't even try to keep a straight face, and busts out laughing. "No, I've got better things to do with my time. We just happen to like the same type of food," he grins.

Ugh, I wish I could slap that look off his face. I glare at him and say, "I'm just gonna get my food, and go. I'll see you later this afternoon."

He moves so that he's blocking me. "I'm not running you off, am I?" He has a twinkle in his eye like he knows that he affects me.

"Nope, I just have stuff to do before we start working on the paper," and I pivot toward the door.

This time he grabs my arm, "Stay and eat with me. What do you have to do before meeting at the coffee shop?"

I'm staring, mouth open in shock. Why does he want me

to stay and eat with him? He acted like I wasn't worth his time yesterday.

I mumble, "I've got to get my supplies for my painting."

He nods like he knew that all along. "I've got to get the pencils and board for my project, too. Maybe I can come with you, and we can talk about the paper while we're getting the stuff. Two birds, one stone, and all of that."

I don't say anything, and he takes this as agreement. He grabs our trays and leads me to a booth.

I've seriously got to start vocalizing. I'm not a person to give in to orders. I may be a good kid, but I don't like being told what to do. Especially by some guy that I don't even freaking know.

He tries to make small talk about the weather and school. But I can't find it in me to be very talkative. I know he's just trying to be nice, but his reaction to me today is completely different than yesterday. He acted like I had the plague, and today he wants to be chatty. Did he have a sudden change of heart about me? Or is he just pitying me for my situation? Guys are so confusing. I do my best to be polite and answer his mundane questions. Once we finish our food and put our trays by the trash can, we walk out of the burger joint.

I start heading toward my car, thinking he'll get into his and meet me at the craft store. I'm wrong. When I look up after unlocking my door, he's standing by the passenger-side door, eyebrows raised, with an expectant look, waiting for me to unlock it for him. I wish I could knock that smug smirk right off his face.

ten

I OPEN the door and get in. He's still standing there, waiting patiently. I roll the window down and say, "What the hell do you think you're doing?"

He stares at me like it should be obvious. "I'm waiting for you to let me in the car." When I continue glaring at him he adds, "I figure we might as well ride together since we are going to the same places. No use in us both wasting gas."

I know he's right, but what comes out of my mouth is, "So we have to use *my* gas?" He shakes his head and tells me he'll fill my car up. I'm not going to let him do that because that seems so petty. Instead I hit the button on the door handle allowing him entrance into my space. How does he continue to get me to do things that I wouldn't normally do?

I reverse out of the parking lot and start toward the street. Reaf is about to get a huge awakening when he realizes how vocal I am when I drive. It's not that I don't think other people can't drive, well maybe it is a little bit, but I get so frustrated with people who act like their time is more

55

valuable than mine and pull out right in front me. It's frustrating, and pisses me off more than it should. Apparently he's realizing this as I see his hand fly up to the "oh shit" handle, and hold on to it for dear life. I hear him mumbling, and say, "Excuse me? What is that you're saying?"

He glances at me shocked that I heard him. He clears his throat, "I said maybe I should have driven myself."

I glare at the road because that's what I was pushing for from the beginning. "Too late now buddy."

We make it to the craft store with all his limbs intact. He acts like I was on a NASCAR circuit. I shake my head and walk toward the doors. I love the craft store. It reminds me of my great-grandmother. I never see her without yarn and a crochet hook. I loved sitting beside her while she worked on her projects. It always amazed me that she could make clothes and blankets out of what amounted to a piece of string. Thinking of those times reminds me that I need to call her and see how she's doing. I love that woman with everything I have.

I could walk the aisles of a craft store for hours, but don't feel like it today since I have company in tow. Glancing back at him, I don't think spending tons of time in here will be a problem. He has that same awe that I have. I wonder what other crafts he's good at besides sketching. These are things I should not be wondering. I call back to him, "I'm going to look at the canvases and paints. Find me when you are ready to go." I don't wait for a reply and make my way to that section of the store. I think I love crafts so much because you can create anything. The possibilities are endless and you can use things in ways other than what they were intended.

I walk over to the wall with the canvases. There are so many sizes, and I'm having trouble deciding which one I want to use. Picasso's version is pretty big, and I don't want to use a canvas that big, but I don't want to make the work microscopic either. I grab a frame that is 18x24. Holding it in my hands I think it's the perfect size, and walk to paints. I am so excited about this project and can't keep my eyes from bouncing to each color laid on the shelf before me. I know what colors I need, but I don't want to just buy the colors I need. There are some that I want to mix. I want to get the tone just right so that it isn't only a recreation of the painting, but also my own. Thompson never said I couldn't change anything, and I plan on adjusting the hues.

I lose time weighing my options with the colors because I see Reaf coming down the aisle out of the corner of my eye. He's got charcoal pencils and a piece of muslin rolled up in his hands. He stands beside me and asks, "Did you forget what colors you're supposed to use?"

I don't even bother with a sarcastic comeback. "Not exactly, I just want to mix my own colors, and I'm having a difficult time deciding which hues I should get." He's on his phone, and I assume he isn't even listening to anything I've just said. When he shoves his phone in front of my face I'm surprised to see he's pulled up an image of my painting. I didn't think he even remembered which one I was doing. I only mentioned it in class, but I guess he was actually paying attention. We spend a few minutes sorting through the colors until we find exactly what I'm looking for. We also grab a palette for me to mix the colors with. If I'm going to do this, I might as well get all the equipment to make it easier for me. Mom would die if I used one of her dinner plates to mix my colors. I pick up a couple of brushes of various widths and we make our way to the checkout line. Luckily, I got paid Friday because art supplies are expensive.

We leave the store and walk toward the Jeep. I'm almost to the driver door when he whips in front of me and demands, "keys."

My mouth falls open. No way in hell is he driving my baby. I don't care if he thinks I'm the world's worst driver, only I am getting behind the wheel. Except Reaf isn't backing down. We look like we are about to duel, and stuck in a standoff. "You aren't driving my car."

He looks like I haven't said anything at all, and still has his hand hanging in the air waiting for me to put the keys in his hand. "I'm not getting back in that deathtrap with you unless I'm driving. We can stand here for the rest of the day for all I care. I don't have anything better to do." I can tell he's serious, and argue with myself in my head. I would gladly wait until he changes his mind but my feet are hurting. And honestly, I'm kind of tired. It's been a long time since I've been out and about like this. I've mostly gone to work, school, and straight home.

I relent and slam the keys into his outstretched hand. "Fine, you drive. But be careful with her, she's needs a little extra TLC."

Reaf huffs. "Yeah, because you are so gentle with your car." I give him the finger and walk around to the passenger side. Pretty juvenile, but I'm tired, and don't have the energy to argue.

We arrive at Brews Clues ten minutes later. Yes, I know it

sounds kind of cheesy since it's a play on that cartoon kids seem to love so much. But I love this place, or at least I did when I was able to come here and get my caffeine fix.

They even have a beautiful royal blue sofa against one wall, and red chairs that are very similar to the ones in the show. There are small café tables spread around for those that come in here to do whatever work needs to be done in peace. Since today I am one of those people, I know I won't be able to relax on that comfortable, plush sofa. Sighing I follow Reaf to the counter. I don't even know what I can drink here since I'm pregnant. Coffee is the one thing the doctor told me I needed to stop inhaling when I went to my first visit. I've managed, but it's been brutal. That may be the reason I'm so irritable and difficult to be around for a long period of time.

I'm salivating from the aroma surrounding me. I think Reaf notices it and asks what I would normally drink when I come. I tell him white chocolate mocha is the only way to go, but I'll take a water since I'm trying to be strict with the doctor's orders.

I turn around and survey the available tables trying to decide which one will be the best and most quiet one to work at. I'm heading to a table in the corner when I hear Reaf call my name. He's pulling a side table in front of the blue sofa so there will be a place to write. Dude is definitely earning brownie points in my book. He's actually got some chivalry under all that bad boy attitude. I don't have to be told twice, and practically skip to the sofa.

"We could have sat at an actual table."

He smiles at me and says, "I figured this would be better

for your back. You've been on your feet a lot and you have got to be exhausted."

My mouth falls open. I actually have no words, so I sit down and get comfy. The barista calls Reaf's name and he gets up to get our drinks. I begin wondering if I look as tired as I feel. Maybe I'm looking rough, and he can tell. That bothers me more than it should. When Reaf comes back to our spot on the couch he's carrying two coffee cups. I open my mouth to protest.

"Don't worry it's decaf," he says. I'm still staring at him like he's got two heads. I don't even know if I can have that.

"When my sister was pregnant her doctor told her she could have decaf coffee sometimes. I was the lucky one that got to go out and get it when she had her cravings." So, he has a sister and a niece/nephew.

"Thank you," I mumble. I take a sip, and even though it's not as strong as what I was used to, it tastes like Heaven. I wonder why my doctor never mentioned this little tidbit to me. I guess she thought I would go crazy on the coffee if she told me I could.

I rummage through my bag and pull out my notebook. I'm happy that I've taken a few notes so we have a starting place. When I set it down on the table, I notice another one already sitting there. I look over at Reaf, and he's grinning like this is some huge accomplishment.

He beams, "I guess great minds think alike."

We begin comparing notes, and work out a general outline for our paper. This is going a lot faster than I thought it would. We've only been here an hour and we have everything we need to ace this assignment. We decide he will write up the paper, and I'll proof read it. I'm a huge procrastinator, and I don't want him constantly bugging me about if I've written the paper yet. But I'm not ready to go home yet. Reaf is extremely easy to work with, and definitely easy on the eyes. He knows his art, and I understand why he wanted to pick Picasso. He starts putting his notebook away, and I just sit back, making no move to put my notebook in my bag.

"Are you ready to head back to my car?" Reaf asks.

"Not really. This is the first time I've been out and actually enjoyed myself in way too long. Why don't we just hang out and chat?" To my surprise Reaf agrees.

I'm not sure where to start this conversation. But he said he had a sister that was pregnant, and inquiring minds want to know. "So, do you have a niece or nephew? You mentioned your sister was pregnant at one time."

Reaf has that look that proud relatives get. You know, the one that is all beaming smiles and bright eyes. He says, "Nephew. His name is David, and he's two."

"Terrible Twos going on around your place? I can honestly say from all the horror stories I've read, that's not a phase I'm looking forward to." I shiver at the thought.

He just laughs. "It's not as bad as people make it out to be. He's actually a lot of fun. He's talking, and running around. And he sees every day like a great big adventure."

Maybe Reaf isn't as "bad boy" as I thought.

We spend the next couple of hours talking about our families, and banal things like our favorite colors. His is black, which I figured with the amount of it he wears. He's shocked to learn that my favorite color is hot pink. He thought I would like some broody color like dark gray. I can't stop myself from laughing at that. Reaf has a sister and a little brother. Caroline is three years older than me. She married her high school sweetheart and they got pregnant soon after. Reaf's brother, Bryce is a freshman this year, and he also goes to Asheville High.

Before I know it the manager is trying to scoot everyone out the door. Wow, we spent this long together talking, and not being awful to each other. This is the most conversation I've had with anyone close to my age, and it feels good to just talk without worrying they are going to pry about the pregnancy and ask a million questions.

I don't bother arguing with Reaf about driving back to get his car. When we get there I still don't want the night to end, but I have to work tomorrow, and finish my homework for calculus. I hate calculus with a fiery passion. Who the hell is actually going to use this crap on a day to day basis?

Reaf gets out of the car and opens the door for me so that I can get back in the driver's seat. This feels very date like. I don't know how I feel about this. There are butterflies squirming around my stomach when he takes my hand to help me out of the car. Am I supposed to shake his hand, wave bye, or hug him. I don't have long to debate because Reaf sweeps me into his arms for a massive hug. It feels nice.

Reaf whispers into my ear, "Thanks for today. It was a lot of fun. Maybe we can do it again sometime, without all the homework."

I'm not sure what to say, so I shrug. "Maybe."

I wave and tell him bye as I'm climbing back into the Jeep. I make my way back home, and walk straight to my room. My parents are already asleep so that they're ready for their long day of work. I change into my pajamas and consider working on my homework before deciding I'll finish it before class. Crawling into bed I think of the way it felt to be in Reaf's arms. I'm still not sure if it's because I haven't been held by anyone in so long, or if I'm actually attracted to him. I'm not going to argue either point tonight, and fall asleep with the thought of Reaf's mouth close to my ear asking if we can go out again.

eleven

THE NEXT WEEK FLIES BY. I haven't seen Reaf since we worked on the paper last weekend. He's obviously not a procrastinator because I woke up Monday morning to see an email waiting in my inbox from him. He did an awesome job of putting our facts together in a way so that it doesn't read like a boring report. There were very few things I had to correct. I emailed him back with the corrections, and I assume he's okay with it because he never sent it back.

We have texted each other quite a few times over the week. Reaf has kept the conversations away from school-work though. Most of them were just crazy pictures he found online trying to get me to laugh. I'll be honest, dude has sense of humor that closely resembles mine. Most of the texts came at night because he knew I had work and school. I'm glad he is considerate enough to realize that I can't reply often during the day. He does seem to have a habit of catching me when my hands are covered in paint, however.

Working on this painting has been therapeutic. It's like I'm pouring all of my fears and anxiety into this project. I feel lighter, and more free. I find myself actually looking forward to this pregnancy more than I have in the months before.

Even my parents have noticed the change in my attitude. They probably think it's because of Reaf. They somehow manage to be around when I get a text from him, and sometimes I can't keep the smile off my face when I hear from him. He's actually a pretty cool guy. He's not at all how I pegged him. I realize I probably shouldn't judge someone from first impressions.

I'm about to put my hand to the canvas when my phone buzzes.

Reaf: What are you doing? Dinner? -R

This is one of those times that I'm happy Mom and Dad are out on a date. They would want answers as to why I have a smile that stretches across my face.

I send a picture of my paint splattered pants.

Me: Can't. I'm working on my painting and I'm a mess. Raincheck?

Five minutes pass, and I figure he won't respond, so I start working on the girl. She's very complex. Not so much in the actual structure of her, but because of the emotion that has to be evident in her expression. It seems like it will be such a difficult thing to replicate, but I've got so many pent up feelings that it just flows. I begin another section of the painting, and my phone goes off again.

Reaf: How about I come over and we can work on our projects together? I can bring food....

There's no way I can resist food. I realize I haven't even eaten since I got home from work. I can't remember the last time that has happened since the cravings started to hit.

Me: Sure. Not picky, just let me know how much I owe you.

I also send him the address because I doubt he knows where I live. We live in a tiny town, but I didn't even know who he was until our art class. I don't understand why he wants to see me so bad tonight. I mean we have class tomorrow, and he'll see me then. I thought these fun texts between us was equivalent to being buddies, despite the tingles that spread across my skin saying otherwise.

Twenty minutes later there's a knock at the door. I glance through the window to make sure it's Reaf. Opening the door, I'm preparing to help him carry whatever he has into the house, but stop because as soon as he sees me, he busts out laughing. This is so not the reaction I was planning on getting.

"What the hell is so funny? I can't look that bad."

Reaf is trying to catch his breath, and says, between chuckles, "You might want to look in a mirror."

So I do just that. I tell him to head to the kitchen off to the right, and make my way to my room and the mirror that takes up almost my entire door. I stare in horror. When I told him I was a mess I assumed I just had paint on my arms and pants. Looking in the mirror shows just how wrong I was. There are smears of color all over my face, and somehow the paint got in my bun. How the hell does that even happen! No wonder he couldn't stop laughing at me, I look like a damn clown. I go to the bathroom and wash my face as best as I can. This paint is going to take some major scrubbing before I go to bed.

When I enter the kitchen, Reaf has cartons of Chinese food set up on the island. Apparently he thinks one single preggo chick can eat all that. I'm so hungry I just might, but I seriously doubt it.

He glances at me. "I didn't know what you wanted so I got a little bit of everything."

I'm amazed, yet again, at his thoughtfulness. I sit on a stool next to him and dig in. I don't bother trying to have a conversation because I am that hungry. He must sense that because he starts eating too. When we're done, and there are still a few leftover cartons to put in the fridge, I show him to the living room. I'm surprised Mom didn't say anything about me painting in here, but I think that's because the floors aren't carpeted, and anything I spill will come up if I get to it fast enough.

Reaf is looking at my painting, whistling. "That is pretty fantastic. Your colors match almost exactly, and you can almost feel the emotion rolling off the canvas."

"Thanks. I was hoping I would be able to make it feel as real as possible. I'm almost done, but I think I want to darken up some of the lines."

He nods his head. "Yeah, maybe make these lines a little wider and bolder. I'll be right back; I'm going to go get my supplies."

"Sure," I reply. I begin doing exactly as he said. It adds so much more to the expression of this piece. I'm not sure why, but it almost brings out how lonely this girl feels.

I hear the door open back up, "I want to see yours!"

Reaf begins rolling out his muslin, and I stare in astonishment. *Guernica* is such a detailed piece. There aren't many colors, but you have to be able to bring the smaller images to the forefront. I can tell he's spent a lot of time on this. I don't see where he found the time with writing the paper, but it's magnificent.

"Why did you need to come over here to work on your project when it's pretty much finished?" I ask.

"I wanted your opinion. I know it seems crazy, but you have an eye for creativity, and I want to make sure I'm capturing the gloom he portrayed in his original."

I nod because there are no words to describe his work. He's shaded every piece the way it needs to be. You can see the outline of the eye, and the destruction in the background. I can't believe he was able to capture all of the detail. He must not sleep *at all*.

Reaf starts darkening up some of the images to make them stand out more than they already do, and I go back to putting the last touches on my painting. It's not due until next Saturday, but this is one thing I didn't want to wait until the last minute to finish. I'm glad I didn't. I don't think it would have turned out as well as it has if I had rushed through it. I'm happy with it, and I glance toward the floor and see that Reaf is rolling up his work.

I don't want him to leave yet. "So do you want to stay and watch a movie or something? My parents are out to dinner, but they should be gone for a while. Not much to worry about when your teenage daughter has already gotten herself into a predicament."

He looks like he's unsure of how to respond, so he nods. I finish putting up the easel, and wash my brushes so they don't become useless. When I get back to the living room I head straight to the entertainment center. I grab the first Harry Potter. It's coming up on Christmas and I always watch them this time of year. I know most people watch them around Halloween because of the whole wizard thing, but these movies are precious and cozy to me. They remind me of Christmas, and I can't go without watching them.

Reaf asks, "Are we having a *Harry Potter* marathon?"

"Yep! I never specified what we would be watching. If you don't like it, well, too damn bad."

He chuckles, "I'm good with some wizardry action. It's been a while since I've seen them."

While we are waiting for the menu to come up on the DVD player, Reaf clears his throat. I gaze at him, and he seems like he's about to ask a very uncomfortable question.

"So, I know this is none of my business, but where is the baby's dad? I figured he would be around."

I groan, I was hoping this question would never come up. But if I'm being honest I need to talk about it with someone.

"I broke up with him the day after graduation. He was a jerk one time too many, and I couldn't take it anymore. Besides, Jake always talked about getting out of this small town, and making something of himself. He had a scholarship for football to a great school, and I didn't want to hold him back. When I told him I was pregnant, he wanted to get back together and I didn't want a child to be the reason that happened. I haven't talked to him since then."

Reaf looks at me like he understands. "So... you aren't seeing anyone?"

That is not the question I thought would come next. He just completely shocked me.

"Nope, not seeing anyone. Why?" I stammer out.

"Well, I happen to know this guy that thinks you are pretty great, and would like to get to know you better, and possibly even go out on a few more dates."

Hold up, did he just say "more dates"? I guess he's counting tonight as a date. Working on school projects isn't exactly something I consider a date-like activity, but I guess he has other opinions on the matter.

I can't stop from grinning, and maybe flirting back. "And would this guy happen to be sitting on my couch getting ready to watch one of the best series in the world?"

Reaf answers with a smile, and puts his arm around my shoulders.

I know I'm not going to tell him no. Talking all week and hanging out with him these couple of times has been great. He makes me smile, and doesn't make me feel like I'm a total loser because I'm pregnant at eighteen. Most people look the other way, or have pity in their eyes when they see me. Reaf doesn't. He treats me like a normal person.

"I think we could work in a few dates. But you have to understand, this chick eats a lot here lately."

Laughing he says, "I know. And just so you know, being pregnant doesn't scare me off. I like you. I noticed you when you walked into class the first day."

"Really?" I ask.

I must have a weird look on my face because he laughs. "Yeah, why wouldn't I? You're beautiful."

Now I'm really confused. "Why didn't you say anything before the project?"

He shrugs. "I don't know. Some days you'd put off a bitchy vibe, but other days you looked like you were happy and didn't have a care in the world. Honestly, it kind of freaked me out. As time went by I noticed the growing baby bump, and thought you might have a boyfriend at home."

Sighing, I play with the ends of my hair poking out of my bun. "Sorry about that. My emotions have been running high the past few months. With the pregnancy, and worrying about my best friend. I guess I don't really make the greatest impressions."

Reaf grabs my hand. "Don't be sorry. We all have shitty days. I'm glad I'm taking the time to get to know you... And date you." He's grinning like this might be the happiest day of his life.

Sighing, because really how perfect of a response was that, I rest my head on his shoulder. "Can we go easy on the heavy topics for a bit, and watch some Potter?"

Reaf grabs the remote out of my hand and presses play.

We must have fallen asleep while the movie was playing. I hear a loud "mmhmmm" sound from right in front of us. I groggily look up to see dad hovering above me. I nudge Reaf's shoulder to wake him up. He jumps, startled. He looks like he's about to make a joke, but he notices the shadow standing over us.

He looks up at my dad. "Uh, hi. I'm Reaf. Tonya and I have been working on the project for art class." I can tell he wants to shrink back. Dad can be pretty intimidating.

Dad glances at me. "So this is the "douchebag" you were ranting about last week?" He makes sure to use air quotes to drive the punch home.

I wish the floor would swallow me whole in this moment. Leave it to my dad to decide he wants to use profane language now.

I look at Reaf, "I'll explain later."

Reaf gives a quick nod, and announces that he's going to leave. As soon as he's out the door my dad whirls on me.

Before he says anything I hold up a finger. "Daddy, I'm really tired right now. Can we talk about this tomorrow when I get home from class?"

I know he wants to argue, but he knows I was obviously tired since he had to wake me up. He nods, and I go past him to my room. I don't even change out of my paint stained clothes. I fall, not very gracefully, onto my bed, and pass out.

twelve

UGH, is that my alarm already? I'll be so happy when I can sleep in on Saturdays again. Then the knowledge that I will probably never get to sleep in again when the baby gets here hits me like a ton of bricks. I groan and fall back on my pillow.

Can't I just skip class today? Knowing I can't since there are only two classes left, I get up and get dressed. My pre-pregnancy clothes stopped fitting a while back. Thank goodness Cami took me clothes shopping before she left. I need to call her. I haven't talked to her in a while and it's starting to freak me out. We were talking every day, and she's pulled back lately. But there's not much I can do about that right now.

I'm heading out to my car, and there's an extra bounce in my step. Not only because I'm already finished with my final project, but because I get to see Reaf pretty soon.

As soon as I round the corner of the house I see Reaf's car sitting in the driveway. I know he said he wanted to go on a few dates, but I didn't think he'd come pick me up for class.

He sees me heading toward his car, and scrambles out of the driver seat.

He must see the look of confusion on my face, "I figured we are going to the same place, and could maybe grab some lunch after."

"Pretty presumptuous of you, don't ya think?" I can't keep the sarcasm out of my voice, I'm hardwired that way.

"I also didn't want to have to talk you into letting me drive. Quite frankly, your driving scares the shit out of me." He has this sheepish look on his face like I'm about to rip it off for insulting my driving. It's not the first time someone has said something about how I handle my vehicle.

I say, "Well, I guess I can ride with you. Can I get in? I'm freezing my ass off out here."

Reaf hurries to the passenger side door to open it for me. I try to hide my grin as he rounds the car to get back in the driver seat. It's the little things that really matter. Grand gestures are nice every once in a while, but I love the simplicity of opening the door for someone.

That was something that Jake never understood. He always had some elaborate thing planned when he wanted to show me how much he cared about me. I would have been just as happy with him giving me a freaking candy bar. It's the thought that counts. I don't really blame him, not completely. His parents always showed their affection by buying massive gifts. I don't think I ever saw them relax around each other. I always felt like their marriage was so formal, like those parents on teen shows. Most people think they act that way because they are wealthy. I completely disagree.

Mom and Dad aren't exactly hurting for money, but they

don't ever take themselves too seriously. There have been times when I'd walk into the kitchen and they'd by dancing with no music, and happier than anything I've ever seen. I would always watch them, and know that I want a relationship like that when I got older.

"Hey Tonya?" Reaf's voice breaks into my thoughts. Was he talking to me this whole time? He gives me a knowing look, and I shake my head in disbelief when he just smiles and starts the conversation over.

"I'm going to go ahead and turn our paper in today if that's okay with you. I'm sure Thompson would like one less thing to grade next week, even though he wouldn't have to grade this if he wasn't being such an ass."

There's a smirk forming on Reaf's lips. He doesn't seem too upset about being forced to do this assignment with me. In fact, he looks pretty happy that we worked on it together.

"Sure," I say. "I mean we might as well since it's done."

Reaf pulls into a parking space, and comes around to open the door for me. I could really get used to this. I practically sprint to the building, well maybe I just run as fast as my growing body will allow me. It's December and freezing. And I don't do cold. I've always thought I should have been born somewhere like Hawaii where it's pretty much the same temperature all year. It's not like it usually gets cold here in Texas, but it seems like this fall/winter, because that's the only way to describe the season, has been brutal.

Reaf quickly catches up. "Are you training for a marathon or something?"

I laugh. "Nope. It's cold out there, and it's warm in here. I'd prefer to be in here."

It seems like the green in his eyes darken when he says, "I know how to keep you warm."

This time I can't control the volume of my laugh. I'm laughing so loud, and hard, that I almost have to bend over to try to get myself under control. "Yeah, okay. Because that's what every guy wants. To get their mack on with the local pregnant girl."

I can't seem to figure out what he sees in me. He's looking at me like I'm the most beautiful and precious thing he's ever seen, but I just don't get it. When I look in the mirror I see a girl with long hair that is so dark it looks almost black. I'm short and ridiculously pale thanks to the lack of sunshine lately. And my stomach is no longer flat like it was just a short time ago. What guy in his right mind, at our age, would think this is any kind of attractive.

Reaf puts his hand under my chin, and moves my head up so that I can see his eyes. "You are beautiful. You practically glow." He knows I'm about to butt in to his little speech so he hurries on, "And no, it's not that pregnancy glow that people talk about. You have a certain spark. It's what caught my interest that first day of class."

I don't even know how to respond to that, or if I can form words that will show just how much what he said means to me. So I wrap my arms around him and give him a tight hug. I lean my head against his chest, and let his embrace calm me. I know we've been standing here for a while, but I don't want to move. I'm wondering if it's too late to decide to skip, but I see Thompson walking down the hall out of the corner of my eye.

"Okay kids, break it up and get to class," he chuckles as he passes us by. So that was slightly embarrassing. But I linger in Reaf's arms a little longer before I step back. I grab his hand and pull him toward the open door.

When we walk into class I take my normal seat at the front. It's closest to the door, and I like leaving as soon as possible. I don't know what I was thinking taking a Saturday class. I figure Reaf will head to the back of the room where he usually sits. But to my surprise he glares at the person next to me, and takes that seat as soon as the guy gets up.

"So, you're a caveman now?" I ask playfully. He just grins.

Thompson stands at the front, behind his podium, and starts in on his lecture. I don't even pretend to listen because I know I'm going to ace this class, especially after I turn in my painting. I begin doodling in my notebook. It's something I've always done when I'm bored. I've gotten pretty good at drawing Marvin the Martian. Although, he's not exactly a tough character to draw. If only I could get his body proportionate. Okay, so I'm good at drawing his head. The body looks more like a Kindergartener got ahold of my paper.

I can feel Reaf watching me, and it's making me nervous. I've had to redraw the circle of Marvin's head a lot. I give up and start drawing random shapes bunched together until you can't tell where each one begins.

Professor Thompson stops talking, and I look up. I'm sure I'm about to get called out because I'm not paying attention. Instead he tells the class we are free to go so that we can have some extra time to work on our final pieces. Since Reaf and I have finished ours we have a full day to do whatever we want. While I'm putting my notebook in my bag, Reaf goes to the podium. I know he's giving him our report. He even put it in one of those presentation folders with the little slide piece that never keeps the papers in the folder. I hate those kind. They are more of a nuisance than anything.

Reaf grabs my hand pulling me out of my seat. "Ready to get out of here?"

I nod and we make our way out to the parking lot. Before we reach the doors Reaf puts his jacket around my shoulders so that I won't have to run to the car. This guy is way too perfect to be real. But I just clutch the sides closer to me and let Reaf lead the way.

I figure we are going to head to a fast food place to eat an early lunch, but Reaf parks in front of an ice cream parlor. Because it's obviously not cold enough. We need to add ice cream to the awful freezing temperature today. I shake my head. He just keeps on amazing me.

"We need dessert after having to sit through that boring lecture. We'll get lunch a little later." He says while I just stare at him.

We walk up to the counter and scan the choices. They have so many different flavors it's unreal. I wait to see what Reaf is going to choose, and know it will give me more insight into who he is. I don't know why I think this, but ice cream choices are personal. You can tell if a person is plain or exciting in what they choose. Reaf gives the teen behind the counter his order: a dish with a scoop of chocolate rum, caramel, and he throws me for a loop when he adds strawberry. The first two flavors he picked are so rich, and he throws in a little bit of sweetness. It matches his personality so well. I place my order: birthday cake in a waffle cone with

M&M's mixed in. I've never had the birthday cake flavor, but it's a bright blue, and the candy just makes it sparkle in all the best ways. Chocolate mixed in with anything is pretty much the best thing in the world.

We find a table in the back corner. It's not like we have to be choosey. We are the only ones in here. And apparently the only ones insane enough to want ice cream when it's barely hit forty degrees today. As soon as my butt hits the seat I dig in. I'm starving since I didn't eat breakfast, and it's just so damn good. I don't think I've ever eaten ice cream in the winter, but it's now my favorite thing to do.

When I've made a pretty good size dent in my ice cream I set it aside. "So, my dad is probably going to ask a million questions when I get home. I think if we are actually going to date and see what happens, then you may need to meet my parents when we aren't sleeping on my couch."

He nods. "Yeah I know. Waking up to your dad glaring at me was pretty fucking scary. Speaking of, why did he call me a douchebag?"

I look away, sheepish. "I may have called you that when I was ranting to my dad about being paired up with you for the paper." He is about to cut in, but I forge on. "You just seemed so pissed and agitated about doing the paper with me. I didn't know what to make of you. So I got angry and figured you were this awful guy, and couldn't be bothered with doing the assignment."

Now he does have something to say. He pushes away his ice cream and begins explaining. "It wasn't that I was pissed. I was a little frustrated that you wouldn't back down and pick someone else. But now I'm glad you didn't. Even with the 'stay away from me' attitude you give off sometimes, I'm completely drawn to you. Why can't you see how bright you shine?"

This guy is definitely in the wrong classes. He should be spouting poetry in the English department. I don't know what to say yet, so I sit there and gather my thoughts.

"You really think that? All the other people in town look at me like I should be pitied. I'm what their children should never be. I thought maybe you thought the same thing when you stormed down the hallway."

He shakes his head. "Nope. You are one of the strongest people I know. You decided to be a single parent. You did what you think is best for you, and for Jake, even though he doesn't realize it yet. That takes a lot of guts."

I feel the weight lift off my shoulder with those words. I worried for no reason. I can see this thing with us possibly going somewhere. I know it's early for that and I am going to take things slow with him, but he makes me feel things that Jake never did.

"Come to dinner on Friday," I blurt out. "I mean, we both agree my parents need to meet you and before we continue to see where things go with us, I really want my parents' support. I know the scene they walked in on the other day was a shock to them, but I want them to get to know you."

He doesn't even hesitate when he asks, "What time?"

"Um, I have no idea. Let me text my mom and see what time she plans to cook."

After sending the text, I just kind of sit there. I went from feeling irritated with Reaf to kind of liking him in just a week. Who does that? I'm not sure if it's pregnancy hormones or what, but I like hanging out with him.

"Tonya, hellooo, earth to Tonya." Reaf is waving his hand in front of my face.

I snap out of my thoughts, and glance at him. "Yeah?"

Reaf just shakes his head. "You had this far off look in your eyes, and your phone went off. You didn't even realize it."

"Oh, I'm sorry. I kind of zoned out." I say

"It's okay. You look kind of tired. Maybe we should cut the day short, and you can go get some rest. Maybe the nights working on your painting are catching up to you." Reaf has this worried expression on his face, and it's the most adorable thing ever.

"Yeah, maybe. I am feeling pretty wiped out," I say as we walk to the door.

I thought this phase wasn't supposed to hit until later on in the pregnancy. Maybe I should start eating better, or something.

It's barely one, and I see my dad peeking out the window when we pull up.

I look to Reaf, "I guess I better go get this over with."

He gives me a quick hug, and waits for me to get out of the car.

Before I close the door, I remember the text Mom sent me about dinner. "Oh yeah, dinner Friday around 7:00. That's when Mom says she'll have dinner ready."

He backs out of the drive as soon as the door shuts. This is obviously not something he wants to be around for. I open the front door, toss my bag on the counter, and prepare to reason with the only man whose opinion has ever mattered to me, until now.

thirteen

I DON'T REALLY WANT to have this conversation but I know it needs to happen. I can already see that Dad isn't going to handle this well, at all. He's standing at the entrance of the living room, arms crossed, stern expression on his face. I can't tell if he's angry, or worried, but I need to do everything I can to assuage his fears.

"Tonya, I'm not too sure this is a good idea," Dad begins. "Coming home to my daughter asleep on the couch with this boy that I don't even know is not how I wanted to end last night. And are you sure you should be seeing someone when you are pregnant? I know this whole thing hasn't been easy, but maybe you should slow down some."

The fact that he's already laying into me kind of annoys me. "Dad, last night we worked on our art pieces, and fell asleep watching Harry Potter. I think we've decided to start dating, but we are going to take it slow. I did invite him over for dinner on Friday so that you can properly meet."

I figure if I want them to treat me like an adult, because obviously that's going to happen shortly, I need to act like one. Maybe if Dad sees this he won't freak out about my decisions so much. He stands there thinking. I can practically see my arguments swimming through his brain.

He sighs, "Okay Tonya, we will meet him and I'll be as nice as I possibly can. But I still don't think this is a good idea."

I run, and put my arms around him. "I know Daddy. You don't want me to get hurt, or do anything that could hinder my future, but it's different with him. He makes me laugh, and we both know that's something I haven't done in a very long time. He looks at me and sees me, not the poor pregnant girl that everyone else sees. Just give him a chance."

Dad seems at a loss for words for a moment. "I love you sweetheart, and I will do my best. I just want you happy."

With that he turns and heads toward the kitchen. I take my bag to my room and prepare to study for the last couple of classes. I've never been a fan of studying. It just takes so much time. But I know if I want to keep my GPA up, I need to ace these finals. I may be a teen mom, or soon-to-be mom, but I will show everyone that I'm capable of being both a mom and awesome student.

I've already reviewed myself to death with Calculus. That's the only class I'm worried about. Everything else should be fairly easy. I haven't had any problems with the assignments, but this stupid math class has been my nemesis. I know I can't finish reviewing this without some kind of help so I go through the house looking for Mom.

She's in the kitchen baking. The scent of pumpkin and sugar surrounding the room reminds me that I haven't had anything to eat since the impromptu ice cream date Reaf took me on after class. She's got cookies cooling on a rack, and I see banana bread and pumpkin bread on plates on the counter. I really hope she's not saving these for anything because I'm about to devour them whole. I grab a knife out of the drawer, and am stopped by my mother slapping me on the wrist.

I'm still staring at my hand when she says, "Not yet. You can have some after dinner."

"But I'm hungry," I whine. "I haven't eaten since right after class."

"There's fruit in the fridge, you can have that," she admonishes.

I'm pulling out an orange and some grapes when Mom says, "So tell me about this boy coming over for dinner on Friday."

I groan. I'm not angry or anything, but Mom tries to treat me like I'm her best friend instead of her being my mom sometimes. It's weird.

"Yeah," I mumble. "His name is Reaf. We have art class together. Yes, he is also the same boy you saw asleep on our couch last night."

When I glance back at her she has this big, goofy grin on her face. It's almost like she's the one that is dating this fabulous new guy. See, weird... But I know it's because she's happy to finally see me putting myself back out there. She constantly tells me that just because I'm pregnant doesn't mean I can't have a social life. I know she's right, but it's just easier for me to stay home and ignore the world passing me by.

I know she's not going to let the subject drop so I grab my snack and head back to my room. I need her help to make sure I have all of my formulas down, but I'm not in the mood to talk about my love life. Or, well, dating life. I never thought I'd say that when I broke things off with Jake.

I get back to my room and see the light on my phone blinking. There are quite a few messages. I start going through them.

> **Cami:** *Hey T! I'm coming home for the Christmas break. Want to veg out? It's been FOREVER!!!! Love ya.*

> **Reaf:** *Do you miss me yet??? ~R*

> **Reaf:** *I guess that's a no since you haven't responded... ~R*

And then the one that throws a wrench in my stomach. I don't want to deal with this, and I'm going to totally ignore it.

> **Jake:** *I'll be back home next weekend. We need to talk.*

It's like everyone decided to text me as soon as I was away from my phone. I type out a quick reply to Reaf telling him that I kind of miss him. But I'm not taking it further than that. He's fun to hang out with, but I don't want to be dependent on him for my happiness. I did that before, and it didn't end well.

Cami's text is refreshing. She contacted me before I put out an APB on her whereabouts. I've been trying to be there for her, but I can only do so much when we're practically a state away from each other. Something is going on with her, and I hope she opens up some when she comes home for the holidays. She skipped coming home for Thanksgiving, and you bet your ass I'm going to grill her about that, too.

I reply back to Cami.

Me: *Absolutely. My house and Buffy marathon?*

I eat my fruit entirely too fast, and lie down for a nap. All the emotions from seeing the text from Cami soothing me.

fourteen

WAKING up early on Sunday is not the plan, but I can't make myself lie in bed, staring at the ceiling, any longer. I really, *really* miss sleeping in—just another way pregnancy has changed my life.

I *should* go in and do some more filing, but I'll be at the office all day after this week. So I think I'll skip it today. Besides, I smell bacon, and the little bean is demanding to be fed.

I get out of bed and slip my feet into my fuzzy, warm Hello Kitty house boots. This wood floor is effing cold in the winter. I learned pretty quickly to keep something for my feet close to the bed.

When I get to the kitchen, Mom is at the stove.

"How many eggs do you want," she calls over her shoulder.

I swear this woman has a sixth sense. How the hell does she do that? I'm beginning to think moms really do have eyes in the back of their heads. I absentmindedly run my fingers under my ponytail, wondering when mine are going to grow in. Then chuckle at my ridiculousness.

"Um, two I guess," I answer. I could probably eat more, but I don't want to hear any wise cracks about eating for two this early in the morning.

As I'm sliding into my chair, Mom sets the plate of food in front of me. It's hard not to dig in with my fingers. That's how hungry I am. Somehow she knows this, and she shoves a fork into my hand. Smart woman.

"So, what do you want me to make for dinner on Friday for your date?" she asks.

"I don't know, Mom. That's days away. And it's not a date. Dates consist of going out. We aren't going out anywhere. Reaf is coming here to see y'all humiliate me."

"Tonya, we aren't going to humiliate you... much." She grins like she is going to do so much more than that. Maybe I should hide the baby pictures.

"Mom, just please don't embarrass me too much. I think I might really like this guy. Even though Dad thinks it's a bad idea."

"Sweetie," Mom starts. "I know you understand why he thinks so. He doesn't want you to get hurt, and right now your emotions are running rampant. We just want to make sure you are comfortable around this guy, and you don't feel any pressure to date him. Or not date him, for that matter. I'm just happy you are out among the living again."

I sigh. "No, Mom... I'm seeing him because I want to. He intrigues me. It's been a long time since I've been around someone that is interesting. And speaking of interesting, Cami is coming over to hang out when she comes home."

Mom is practically jumping with joy. "Oh, my gosh,

that's amazing, hon. I've missed having her around here. Maybe things will get back to how they were before she left."

"That's the plan," I say. "I miss her more than I thought I would. And she's started pulling away, and I don't know why."

"Don't try to pry too hard, or you may make her shut down. You know how dramatic she can be sometimes, and her controlling father doesn't help matters. I'm just happy she'll be here to visit."

And with that, the conversation is over, and my food is gone. That's the thing I love about my mom. She knows what to say, and when it needs to be said. I hope I'm half as awesome as her when Little Bean is older.

Since I don't have anything else to do, I'm going to relax in my room for the rest of the day. I need some music to help me clear my thoughts about Reaf, Cami and what I'm going to do about Jake. I didn't mention that text, because I'm kind of worried about what my parents will say.

I put the alternative station on Spotify, and get lost in the music. It's one of the few ways I can mellow out, other than reading and binge watching TV shows. The only bad thing is, listening to these bands makes me want to go see them live. I'm not sure my doctor would be okay with me going to any kind of concert. A girl can dream though.

Young the Giant is on, and I've almost been lulled to sleep, when my music is interrupted by a notification.

It's from Jake, of course.

Jake: *Can you talk?*

Me: *Not really. Helping the parents with Christmas decorating.*

Yes, I know I'm lying to him, but I'm in a happy place right now. I don't feel like getting into any kind of conversation with him.

Jake: *Ok, we'll talk when I get home.*

I'm not looking forward to that either. I know I need to talk to him about everything, but if I'm being honest, I just wish he'd leave me alone and not ask questions.

I'm not going to be able to doze off again, so I make my way to the living room. Mom is searching for her keys, as usual. She needs a damn beeper on them so she can find the stupid things.

"You know, Mom, if you would put the keys on the hook you would always know where they are."

She jumps and screams, "Dammit, Tonya! You know I hate when you do that sneaky ninja crap."

All I can do is grin. "So, where ya going?"

"Oh," she says. "I'm going to get your dad's Christmas present and then groceries."

"Do you mind if I tag along?"

"Not at all. Go get ready while I try to find my blasted keys. I refuse to go ask your father for his copy. I'll never hear the end of it."

I know exactly what she means. Dad gets a kick out of being right. Especially when it comes to lost keys. He bought her a key hook, and hung it up right by the door, to prevent this very situation.

I take a quick shower and throw on my yoga pants and hoodie. I'd wear my house boots too if I thought Mom would let me get away with it. Instead, I grab my Converse before picking up my phone and wallet.

Mom is standing by the door, waiting silently. We get in her car and prepare to get our shop on. She knows I'm not one for small talk, or the country music she listens to, so she turns the radio to our local alternative station. She really loves me.

On the ride to the mall, I try to recall the last time we did this. I'm pretty sure it was when I needed to pick out my prom dress. I haven't gone out with her since then because I didn't want to see the shame on her face when others gave her disapproving glances. It would be my fault that emotion was there, since I'm the one that got myself into this mess.

When we get to the mall and are among other shoppers, I know I shouldn't have worried at all. When various people give a sad shake of their heads in our direction, she doesn't look ashamed at all. I think I see pride on her face. I'm not sure why this surprises me, but it does. She obviously doesn't care what others think about me. I've noticed that Reaf doesn't either. Maybe I should take a page from their books and say, "Screw them and their judgey ways."

Shopping for Dad is relatively easy. Mom gets him a new watch, and I buy him a crazy patterned tie. I don't think he really likes the bold colors I pick out for him, but he wears them anyway because he knows it will make me happy.

Just before we reach the exit doors of the mall, Mom veers to the left...straight into a baby store.

* * *

Of all the places Mom decides to take on this mall adventure, she would have to pick the one place I don't want to go right now. I know I'm being enlightened with all the awesome feelings those around me are giving. I'm not quite as terrified to be having this little bean anymore, but I'm still putting off opening the envelope the doctor gave me. Being here will only cause Mom to pester me about it.

I've already lost her, and decide I'm going to peruse the area around me. There are rows of baby beds neatly lined in so many styles. Although I haven't given much thought to decoration, I already know I want a modern style for the nursery. But I also want to make it fun. If my parents wouldn't freak out, I would absolutely turn the nursery into a scene from *The Nightmare Before Christmas*. It's an all-time favorite of mine, and my mind is already spinning with various possibilities.

Who would have thought that a few encouraging words from Mom and Reaf would make me feel so comfortable with planning a nursery. I continue walking down the various aisles, and see a few things I like. I know the whole gothic looking décor won't happen, but I've seen a few things that I like. They are bright blues, pinks, and reds.

Maybe it's time I opened the envelope. I think I will, but I will wait until Christmas to make it more special for my family. I know it'll be the best present I can give my mom. With a plan in mind, I start looking for those "grandma" shirts it seems every grandparent has.

I'm going to have to make this a covert mission. It's kind of hard to get this done with my mom, since the gift is ultimately for her. I walk to the front of the store and grab a basket. The search begins.

After about fifteen minutes I finally find the shirts. Why do some of them have to be so freaking tacky? I mean who wants a pink shirt with bright orange letters saying "Proud Grandma," definitely not me. It just doesn't seem like a good life decision. Sliding hangers across the rack, I finally find one that isn't horrible. It's a white crew neck T-shirt with green, sparkley letters spelling Grandma across the front. It's not gaudy either. It's simple, and gets the message across. I know she's going to love it.

Now it's time to add a few other things to the basket to hide this amazing Christmas present I've found for my amazing mother. I'm in the "essentials" aisle, and putting a few packages of bibs over the shirt. They are the ones with cute little sayings, and gender neutral. Just as I place the last set of bibs covering the evidence, my mom walks toward me. She's got an armful of toys that I'm sure the kid won't use for at least six months.

"Well, I'm glad you are finally buying some things. I don't think you'll need that many bibs at first, though." She says this with a gleam in her eye. I think I've just made her the happiest Grandma in all of existence.

"Since you're here, and judging my purchases, can you help me pick out bottles? I don't know which ones to get, and there are so many choices." I say almost too quiet for her to hear.

"Oh honey, absolutely. There definitely wasn't this selection when I had you, but I'm sure we can find the perfect bottle for this baby." She's grabbing me by the shoulders, and looks like she's about to death hug me.

We finally end up adding some short, bulbous bottles to my basket. They say something about venting to keep the baby from sucking down air when they are drinking. I make sure when we get in line to check out that I choose a different line. I don't want her getting all snoopy trying to see what all I'm buying.

We walk out of the store, and I remember that Cami is going to be at the house over Christmas break. "Hey Mom, can we swing by the Bath and Body store before we head out? I want to grab a few things for Cami."

"Sure thing! I need to get a few things for her too. She *is* practically my other daughter," she says.

Walking into Bath & Body Works, the aroma is almost overwhelming. I loved this store when I wasn't pregnant, but the onslaught of scents is making me sick to my stomach. This is going to have to be a quick purchase.

I grab a few of the flowery bath gels and bubble bath bottles that Cami loves so much, check out and make a speedy exit. A few minutes later, I can see my mom coming through the doors.

"You ready to head home?" She asks.

"Yep. That store was a sensory overload. I'm ready to go home. I still need to finish reviewing for my Calculus final. Any chance you want to help me out with that? It hates me, and I don't think it realizes that the feeling is mutual."

"Sure thing sweetheart."

I hope I never get too old to enjoy her names for me. And I wonder if this is another one of those "mom genes" I'll get when Bean is here.

fifteen

IT'S STARTING to get late. I have to work tomorrow, and I'm not really feeling it. Mom grilled me with math questions until she went to bed. I know I asked for her help, but she didn't have to go all drill sergeant on me.

I'm just about asleep when my phone starts ringing, rather loud. I could have sworn I put it on mute before climbing into bed. I pick it up with such force I almost rip the charging cable out of the wall. As soon as I hit accept, I hear Cami already talking so fast I don't think she's breathing.

"Cami, you need to slow down," I say. "Why are you so damn excited, and why are you calling me so late?"

She finally slows down. "Sorry, I'm just so stoked about getting to see you after FOREVER. How can you not be as excited as I am?"

"First of all, it's 11:30. And I was almost asleep. So that explains my total lack of excitement. Second, couldn't you call tomorrow?"

"Absolutely not," she squeals. "I get to see you in less

than a week. I'm coming over Friday as soon as I come into town."

"That's not going to happen," I retort.

"And why the hell not? I haven't seen you in months. I need my best friend time. I've been going crazy without you." I can hear the disappointment in her voice.

"Because I have plans, dork. I know shocker, but I can't break these."

"I see... Do these plans involve a guy?" Cami inquires. I can hear her voice get all suggestive. This is so not what I need.

"Possibly, but you aren't getting any more information tonight. I'm tired, and have to get up for work in a few hours." I whine. I know she's going to push for more, but I'm too tired to get into all of it.

"Uh uh girlfriend. I need details. How can you not tell me? This is what I'm here for." She has a stern tone.

"That little angry voice you're using right now isn't going to work," I say. "I promise I'll fill you in when you get home. How about you come over Saturday, and I'll tell you everything."

She sighs. "Okay, I guess that will work, but be prepared for questions. And you have to answer all of them. You can't wheedle your way out of it, or change the subject."

"I promise I'll answer everything you throw my way. I'm going to go to sleep now. Night, hon."

"Goodnight, I'll see you bright and early Saturday morning," she says before I hang up.

* * *

Monday morning comes way too fast. Although, I'm pretty excited about it being the last week of the semester. Cami's little late night call has me completely exhausted.

Luckily I'm only working a half day today. Mom wanted to make sure that I get the rest of my studying done. The calculus test is tomorrow and I need to make this test my bitch. I still don't see the point in this class. I've decided it's just to torture the poor souls that hate math. I'm about to get in the shower when I hear my phone ping.

> **Reaf:** *Good morning, Beautiful.*
> **Me:** *Morning. Why are you texting me so early?*
> **Reaf:** *I just figured I'd see what you're up to. And I'm heading to work.*
> **Me:** *I'm getting ready for work. What time do you get off?*
> **Reaf:** *6, why?*
> **Me:** *Wanna meet at Brew's Clues and help me study?*
> **Reaf:** *That depends...*
> **Me:** *It's for my calculus test tomorrow. Do you want me to face the humiliation of not passing and looking like an inept mother???*
> **Reaf:** *It sounds hellish. And we can't have you look like an awful mother for not passing a ridiculous math class. 6:15 work?*
> **Me:** *Perfect. Have an awesome day.*
> **Reaf:** *You too gorgeous.*

Wow, that's probably the longest conversation I've ever had with someone I might be sort of dating. I didn't even carry on long text messages with Jake. And when we were together not much was said. Another indicator of why we would have never worked.

After turning on the water for my shower, I look in the mirror. The reflection is a girl that looks radiant. And happy. So different from how I looked just a few short weeks ago. I can't help the small smile that turns my lips upward. The way I feel right now reminds me of those cute little cartoon characters with hearts in their eyes. What can I say? This ruggedly handsome guy melts the jagged pieces of my cold heart.

I have to make my shower quick. Talking to Reaf took up way too much time this morning. I grab an oversized sweater and a pair of maternity pants out of the closet and put them on. My hair goes up into a messy bun. There's no time to blow-dry it, or do anything with it really.

I rush into the kitchen to grab a package of Pop Tarts and collide into Mom.

"Hey, slow down Turbo," she says.

I stumble back. "Sorry Mom."

"You ready to go," she asks.

"I'm, uh, going to take my car today." I stammer out.

Mom just nods and starts to walk out. "I guess this means you won't be home for dinner..." She sighs, "just make sure you are home at a decent time. I want you well rested for your final tomorrow.:

I smirk. "I will be. It's not like I can get knocked up." The glare she shoots my way lets me know just how not funny she thinks I am.

I don't feel like coming back to the house just to go back to the area I work, so I grab my book and notes before leaving.

My morning consists of filing and paper cuts. I'm beginning to think paper cuts could be used as a form of torture. They sting, and make it almost impossible to bend my fingers.

I haven't seen Mom all day, but when I walk into the break room, I see a takeout container with a note stuck to it.

Had to go meet a client. Brought you lunch. Enjoy the rest of your day off studying.

I shake my head. She really is an amazing person. Opening the container, the smell of chicken fried rice has my mouth watering. She knows my soul. This is just the little energy boost I need to get me through my study session.

I open my textbook and try to study. But all the equations are blurring together. So I push it away and pull a book out of my bag. It's a gothic horror, and I'm stuck inside the world for so long that I don't realize the darkening sky. It's one of the things I hate about the whole time change thing. I'm still trying to get used to it.

Reaf texts me letting me know he's on his way to the coffee shop. Thank goodness, or I'd be super late. I throw everything in my bag and lock up before getting in my car. I'm actually really nervous to meet Reaf for our date. I mean, study session. Putting my car in reverse, I wonder if I'll actually get any studying done.

sixteen

MY HEART IS BEATING INSANELY fast as I pull up to the coffee shop. I've never been nervous around a guy. If anything I was always one of them. It was the same with Jake. Even though I was his girlfriend, I was always one of the guys. Someone they could be obnoxious around, and not get offended.

It's different with Reaf. He makes me feel like I'm on cloud nine. I have things in common with him. We both like art, and we seem to find things to talk about. Even if they are slightly absurd, or simple. He doesn't treat me like I'm an accessory, and I appreciate that more than anything.

I guess I've been sitting in my car for too long because he's walking out of the coffee shop. He pulls open the passenger door, and slides into the seat.

"So, are you going to sit in here for the rest of the night, or are you going to join me inside where it's nice and toasty?" He has this adorable smirk on his face. It's like he's trying not to smile, but failing miserably.

"Yep, I'm coming," I say. "Thank you for reminding me that's it's freezing out here."

I turn off the car, and scramble out as I try to grab my backpack from the back seat. Reaf, the gentleman that he is, grabs the bag out from under my hands and hoists it on his shoulder after shutting the door. He makes it so easy. I mean, I could have just opened the back door, but where's the fun in that.

When we walk in, I notice he's got a table pulled up to the super comfortable sofa again. And there are two mugs of steamy goodness sitting on the table waiting for consumption.

"Do I get another decaf today?" I ask.

"Nope. I figured you could use some hot chocolate. Anything as stressful as calculus deserves chocolate."

Those kind of statements are ones that are going to win my heart completely. I honestly can't figure him out. There's no way he's this sweet all the time. I'm kind of scared to get my hopes up that he's as amazing as he's been.

"You really know the way to a gal's heart," I say, and bat my eyelashes.

He just starts laughing. I love that he gets my sarcasm. Not a lot of people do, and it comes off as me being bitchy. But to each their own.

"How about we get started on this madness, and then we can grab something to eat." He sets my backpack on the couch next to me.

We only manage about an hour of studying. He's surprisingly good at this math stuff. I'm usually pretty decent in math, but something about calculus doesn't click for me. Reaf has given me a few ways to help remember the formulas. He also writes them all down so I have them during the test. Thank goodness Ms. Potts is allowing us to bring a cheat card. As long as it fits on that stupid little rectangle we can use it.

I stand up, and stretch my knotted up muscles out. I'm ready to get out of here. I'm hungry, tired, and just over all the studying. If I don't have it down now, there's no hope for me.

"So, are you hungry?" I ask. "Because I'm starving"

"Sure, where do you want to go?"

"Sonic, I could really go for some cheese tots right now. And Baby Bean is demanding it." I say with a wry smile.

We take his car to Sonic, and order our food. I figured we were going to stay there and eat, but he starts backing out as soon as we get our food.

"Where are we going?" I ask. Like I said before, he has to have some kind of flaw, and I'm hoping it's not that he's a secret ax murderer.

"My house. I don't want to sit in the car and eat. And I want you to meet my nephew." He says.

He looks like he's about to have a panic attack, so I nod and take a drink of my soda.

Ten minutes later we are pulling up to a small blue house. It's cute. The windows are outlined with a white painted frame, and the door has a silver wreath hanging in the middle of it.

I thought I was nervous before, but now that feeling is doubled. What is Reaf's family going to think about him seeing me? Not many parents would be thrilled about their son dating a girl who is about to have the huge responsibility of a child. I'm not sure who all I'm going to meet tonight, but it's time to put my game face on.

He opens the door, and I have all the food in my hands. As soon as we walk in, there is a small boy running up to Reaf with his arms open wide. I can only assume this is his nephew. He's absolutely adorable with his sandy blonde hair, and big brown eyes.

Reaf turns around with this tiny bundle of energy in his arms. "Tonya, this is my nephew, David. Davie, this is Tonya, my girlfriend."

My mind is stuck on the fact that Reaf introduced me as his girlfriend, and I don't see David's fist hanging midair for a few seconds. I look at Reaf with my eyebrow raised.

"He wants a fist bump," Reaf says with a grin.

"Oh, okay. Um, where do I put this food, so I can oblige young Mister David?"

"Follow me."

We make a left into a quaint kitchen. It's small, but cozy. The walls are a light gray, and it gives the room a welcoming feeling. Not too dark to make the room seem smaller, but just enough to open it up some.

I set the food on the kitchen counter, and turn with my fist held out. David bumps his fist against mine, and it actually kind of hurts. This kid has some power behind that small exterior.

Reaf puts David on the floor and starts pulling the food out of the bags. I wondered why he got an extra order of tater tots, but now I know why. He hands the carton to his nephew, and David scampers off to wherever he came running out of when we came in.

I nod in the direction David ran. "So, that's your nephew? He seems very energetic."

He chuckles. "Yep, that's him. He keeps everyone here on their toes. He gets into everything so we've had to put anything breakable where he can't reach it."

"You mean this is what I have to look forward to in a couple of years? Is it bad that I kind of hope I have a mellow kid?" I'm only half joking when I say this.

"By then you'll get used to it. Let's eat, and then we can go to my room."

* * *

Most girls would assume that a guy is trying to get frisky with them by inviting them to their room. But Reaf sits at his desk and lets me plop down on his bed. I can tell he doesn't want to make me feel awkward and it's kind of funny.

I take a moment to look around his room. There are art prints all over his walls. Everything from realism to a print of *Guernica* hanging above his bed. The room isn't a mess like I thought it might be. It's very neat. Everything has a place.

I take my shoes off, and bring my knees as far up to my chest as I can with my protruding belly. "Your sister and nephew live with you?"

"Yeah, it was only supposed to be temporary, but my mom has gotten used to them being around. And I think she may freak out if they try to move. Things didn't work out with Caroline and David's dad, so Mom made sure they had a place to live."

"Wow, your mom sounds pretty amazing." I say. "What about your dad?"

Reaf's face changes completely. He frowns and says, "He took off not long after Bryce was born. I guess he couldn't handle being a parent anymore. I was still pretty young, but from what Mom says things weren't always great. I think that's why she pushes for Caroline to make sure David has a close relationship with his dad, Nathan."

Reaf's mom is definitely someone I already have respect for, and I haven't even met her yet. I kind of hope when I do finally talk to Jake that we are able to keep things cordial. But I'm not sure if that will ever happen, unless he's grown up some this semester.

"That's pretty honorable. Sounds like a smart woman." I say. I'm not sure what else to say to that.

I change the subject instead. "Are you nervous about meeting my parents Friday night? I've already told them not to be completely evil. But don't expect much from my dad. He's not taking me seeing you very well. He doesn't think it's a good idea. I'm kind of scared of what your mom is going to think about you dating a pregnant chick. That's definitely not something most guys our age are known to do."

"She's actually really excited to meet you. I've told her all about you. Maybe you can come here for dinner one night when she's off work. Maybe after Christmas?" He has a slight wobble in his voice like he's afraid I'm going to say no.

"I'd like that. I'm not doing much during break. Cami is coming over while she's home from school. Just be prepared to deal with her soon. She was already asking a million questions when I told her I couldn't hang out with her Friday night."

He laughs. "I can't wait to meet her. I know how this whole 'bestie' thing works. If she doesn't like me then there's no chance in hell you'll go on any more dates with me."

I do a weird combination of laughing and yawning. Reaf takes that as his clue to get me back to my car.

"Let's go, so you can get some sleep," he says while grabbing my hand to pull me off his bed.

I stumble into him while trying to get my footing. My hands are on his chest, and his hands are settled on my waist to keep me from falling. I look up, and his face is inches from my own.

He leans down, and our lips meet. The kiss is soft, sweet, and full of everything first kisses should be. He pulls away, and I lay my head on his shoulder. I sigh, contented. I know exactly what my dreams are going to entail tonight, and I already can't wait for our next kiss.

seventeen

I CAN'T BELIEVE it's already Friday. This week has flown by, and I'm officially done with school until January. I thought the math final was going to kill me, but I have a good feeling about it. I hope Ms. Potts puts the grades up soon. I'm anxious to see my final grade.

Cami has been relentless in her text messages this week. She wants to know the details of this mystery guy that is coming for dinner. And I'll tell her, but not yet. I want to see how tonight goes first.

In just a few short hours Reaf will be coming over to meet my parents. I'm equal parts excited and scared shitless. I don't know what to expect. I know Mom will be super welcoming and as sweet as she always is. It's Dad that I'm worried about. He's trying because he knows this will make me happy. But I also know that he is going to grill Reaf.

I just hope Reaf is able to hold his own. Dad can get pretty fierce when it comes to me. And it's going to be worse since there's also a grandchild to consider. I'm not sure how this is going to play out.

Mom and I went to the grocery store to get things for dinner. I chose spaghetti since it's not hard, and cleanup is pretty quick. And okay, maybe because it's a little romantic even though we are eating with my parents.

* * *

I'm helping Mom and pulling the garlic bread out of the oven when I hear a commotion from the front door. It's almost time for Reaf to get here, but I hear two voices. One of which, I don't want to be hearing right now.

Running to the door, I fling it open and find Jake bowing up to Reaf. Who isn't backing down. Jake looks like he's about two seconds from punching Reaf in the face, and I can't let that happen.

"Dad," I yell. "You better get out here pretty quick."

He must have been on his way to find out what the yelling is because he's by my side as soon as I call for him. He grabs Jake by the shoulder, and tells him to wait on the porch, and asks Reaf inside.

With a stern look on his face Dad says, "Tonya, you need to deal with this, now."

"Okay, I've got this. Can you grab my jacket for me, and get Reaf situated... and calmed down?"

He nods and goes back inside. A few seconds later he's back with my jacket before disappearing into the house.

I shove my arms through the sleeves. "What in the hell are you doing here?" I'm about ten seconds from a panic attack. I knew I would have to deal with Jake, but I didn't expect him to show up on my doorstep unannounced.

He looks indignant. His mouth forming a straight line, and not amused by my shrieking. "Who's that guy?"

It's my turn to bring on my bitch face. "He is none of your business. Now, why are you here?"

He looks like he has more to ask, but I put my hand up in front of me. "Look, we are going to have to talk about this later. I have plans tonight. But I can meet you somewhere tomorrow morning to discuss things."

"Why the fuck can't we talk about this now? I tried texting you, but you never replied. I knew this is the only way you would talk to me. I'm not going anywhere." He says all this while running his hands through his blond hair.

"I'm not going to argue with you right now. And I'm not talking to you tonight when you have this whole temper tantrum thing going on. If you don't leave, I'll just have to call my dad back out here. Is that how you really want this to go?"

His hands are clenched at his side. "Not really, but tomorrow we are talking."

"Noted," I say. I'm trying to keep my own temper in check, and my body is thrumming with energy. It's moments like this that I wish I could run inside to hide from my problems. Cami would have faced this head on, and not had a problem dealing with it right here and now. I'm such a coward.

I stand in the doorway as I watch him walk away. I'm already dreading tomorrow. Cami is going to get an earful from me when she gets here for our sleepover.

When I walk back inside I can feel the tension radiating off of Reaf. "I take it you weren't expecting him?"

I sigh. "Not at all. I'm sorry if he said anything to piss you off. He has no right to come here and act like an ass. And sorry it's kind of made meeting my parents awkward."

He shrugs, and I can see the stress falling off him. "It's fine. If I'm going to date you, I'm going to have to get used to the idea of him being around. Might as well start now. But next time he spews hateful things about you, I will deck him."

"Wait, what did he say about me?"

"I'm not going to tell you. It would just ruin whatever we can make of tonight, and I prefer not to think about it right now."

"I'm not going to get the answer out of you, am I?"

He shakes his head, and grabs my hand. "So, can I officially meet your parents?"

I pull him toward the kitchen, where I'm sure my dad is telling Mom about what transpired outside. And I have my confirmation as soon as we walk into the kitchen. Mom quickly shushes Dad, and puts her hostess smile on.

"So, Mom this is Reaf. Reaf this is my mom, Lucia. And my dad, Jason."

They take turns shaking each other's hands. Reaf wins brownie points with Dad when he addresses them as Mr. and Mrs. Burgess. Dad nods his approval to me, and Mom giggles like a school girl. I roll my eyes at her ridiculous reaction.

We sit around the table, and begin twenty questions. I tried to warn him that this would happen.

"So, what are your plans with school?" Dad asks. He goes straight to his concerns.

"I hope to finish getting my Associates in Art within the next year. Then I'll apply to a university."

"Do you work?" This one from Mom.

"Yes ma'am. I work down at Small Town Automotive. It's not exactly what I pictured doing while attending school, but I'm doing what I can."

Mom seems to like his answer. I think she's just happy that he has a job, and won't be mooching off me.

Now Dad starts to begin his overprotective questions. "What are your intentions with my daughter? And why are you dating her considering she's pregnant?"

Reaf looks momentarily stunned, but then he clears his throat. "Well, Sir, I've liked Tonya for a while. Even before she knew that I liked her. I like to think that this project bringing us together is fate. And while I don't exactly believe in it, I figured why not give it a shot. I know her emotions are everywhere right now, but I'm not going to let that deter me."

I can't keep myself from blushing, or the smile that spreads across my face. I duck my head down so that nobody can see the giddy joy that statement makes me feel.

My dad, however, is relentless. "You realize that she is going to have a baby in a couple of months, right? Do you plan on ending this thing before then, or do you plan to stick with her, knowing the child isn't yours?"

Reaf doesn't miss a beat. "I understand your concern, but I'm willing to be with Tonya for however long she will have me, and as whatever she needs me to be. Even if that is only a friend to lean on. I really like her and will do what I can to make sure she is happy, and appreciated. That includes the little one she's carrying."

At that, Dad is speechless. I am too, to be honest. Jake was the only real relationship I've had, and he didn't show half the sincerity that Reaf has in just the few weeks we've spent together. Maybe there is another chance at romance for me. Even if I feel like a bloated blimp most days.

The evening winds down, and I know that tomorrow is going to be one hell of a day. I lead Reaf to the door to tell him goodnight, and he surprises me by leaning in for a kiss. I don't even think twice before I pull him closer and run my hands through his hair. I can't help deepening the kiss. It's been so long since I've had any physical reaction to a person I'm attracted to that I might be going a bit overboard.

Reaf breaks the kiss and leans back against the wall. "Wow. That went to the next level pretty fast. But it was amazing. Goodnight, Tonya. I'll talk to you tomorrow."

I'm breathless as I tell him, "Text me when you get home so I know nothing happened."

With that he nods and begins walking to his car. I lean against the door brushing my fingers against my lips and trying my best to ignore the butterflies swarming my stomach.

I need to text Cami and let her know plans for tomorrow have changed yet again.

eighteen

AFTER A NIGHT OF FITFUL SLEEP, I'm
exhausted. I was hoping to be at a normal level of function-
ality before meeting with Jake today, but I can see that isn't
happening. I don't know why I'm so nervous. I know he has
the right to know everything, but I'm not ready to hash the
whole situation out with him. I can only imagine what his
buddies have told him, and I'm sure it's not good.

I wish Cami was going with me. She's my best friend
and one of the only people that can give me the strength to
get through this day. I should text her. Maybe she can give
me a quick pep talk so that I don't let my guard down.

> **Me:** *Hey girl, I need your words of wisdom right
> about now.*
> **Cami:** *What knowledge am I doling out?*
> **Me:** *Meeting with Jake in a few. Long story...I'll fill you
> in later.*
> **Cami:** *Put your bitch face on, and don't let him soften*

you up.

Me: That's it? That's your sage advice?

Cami: Pretty much. It's early. You know I'm not at my best in the mornings.

Me: Of course, how could I forget?

Cami: Duh!

Me: Come over this afternoon? You can be my shoulder to cry on.

Cami: Absofuckinglutely. I need out of this house already.

Me: It's a date. Thanks love.

Cami: Anytime hon. See you later.

So that was pretty much pointless. But I know her brain isn't functioning this early in the morning. She's one of those that you don't even bother talking to for at least two hours after she's gotten out of bed. But I'll do my best to keep her fierce attitude as my source of energy today.

I guess it's time to put my big girl panties on and deal with the shit storm that's brewing. I grab one of the muffins Mom made off the counter and walk as slowly as possible to my car. I wonder if I would get pulled over for going below the speed limit on the way to Brew's Clues. I'm seriously contemplating taking the risk.

Asheville is still waking up as I pass the houses with their Christmas decorations still lit up from the night before. I should drive around this time of day more often. It seems like a perfect time to reflect upon one's life. Who am I kidding? If it were up to me, I'd still be sleeping under my comfy blanket. But I told Jake he would get answers, and a public space is the best option. He can't make a scene, and it's early enough that there won't be a ton of people around to witness it.

When I text Jake with a time and place last night before bed, he tried to talk me into coming to my house. I knew right away that was a bad idea. If we were at my house, things have the possibility of getting a little too cozy.

As I pull into Brew's Clues I can see Jake's car sitting in the parking lot. I pull into a spot a few spaces over. I don't want to give him the chance to corner me when we leave, and I will wait him out inside the coffee shop if I need to.

Getting out of the car, I take a deep breath, and muster all the confidence I can. This can go one of two ways, and I've got to be prepared for both of them. Time to get this done.

As soon as I walk in, Jake stands up and walks toward me, two coffee cups in hand. He looks just as bad as I do. I feel a tingle of guilt at the fact that I've done this to him, but I can't let that weakness show. I have a feeling he's going to want to get back together, and even though it's probably the right thing to do, I don't know if I can. I don't really have those types of feelings for him anymore, but I can see myself slipping back into that relationship so easily. And there's Reaf. I want to see how things progress with him.

I stop a few feet from him. I'm terrified of getting too close to him. I don't want him to feel like he has any right to pull me into an embrace. He completely surprises me by respecting my new boundaries for him. Instead of trying to put his hand on my back like he used to, he gestures toward a table in the back corner. This is the first big difference I see between Jake and Reaf. Reaf always takes me to the super comfortable couch.

As soon as we are both seated, Jake pushes one of the coffee cups toward me. "I got your usual," he says.

My usual is a white chocolate mocha, and since I've started this journey to be a mom, I've pretty much banned the stuff. Except the one time Reaf got me a decaf version.

I shake my head. "I can't drink that. The doctor says that too much caffeine is bad for the baby."

His face drops, and he looks like I just punched him in the gut. I feel bad bursting his bubble. I know he was just trying to be considerate and I don't like that I just made him feel like shit.

I grab the cup. "I'm sure this one time won't hurt, though."

There's a brief silence before I ask, "So, where do we start?"

"Who was that guy last night," he asks.

I wasn't prepared for that to be his first question, and I'm not sure how to broach this subject. "That was Reaf. I'm kind of dating him."

His face goes from inquisitive to pissed in point two five seconds. "What do you mean you're dating him? How can you date him while you are going to have my child?"

I take a few moments to keep my own anger in check. "My personal life isn't really any of your business anymore."

Shaking his head, he takes a deep breath. "Okay, I'm sorry. That probably shouldn't have been my first question. But I was hoping that when I came back and we could talk that maybe we could work things out. I want to do what's right. I want our child to have a family. And I want to be a part of that. You pushed me out when I tried talking to you about it before, and didn't give me much of a choice. I should have been the one to decide whether I was ready for fatherhood."

I'm sure my face shows my shock at his statement. Should I have given him the chance to make the choice? Absolutely, but I didn't. It wasn't all because of his scholarship and knowing he wasn't ready. I was still pretty upset with how he handled things after the bonfire. But I didn't expect him to own up to it.

"I don't know if I can do that, Jake. We weren't really great for each other then, and I don't know that we will be now," I say.

Jake reaches across the table and puts his hand over mine. "How do you know if we don't try?"

He has such an earnest look on his face. His eyes sparkle with hope. I shouldn't be conflicted, but I am. Is what I feel for Reaf just my hormones being out of whack, and being happy that a guy finds me attractive at seven months pregnant? Do I pull the brakes on that and see if Jake and I can work through our differences? I'm so confused. Where is my Cami strength when I need it?

I slowly pull my hand out from under his, and start to stand. "I...I can't do this right now Jake. I need time to think."

I don't say anything, or give him a chance to argue his point. I grab my purse from around the chair and head toward the door.

Just as I'm about to open it, Jake calls out. "Are we having a boy or girl?"

I mouth, "I don't know."

I push the door open with tears making tracks down my cheeks.

nineteen

THE DRIVE HOME is proving to be difficult with tears blurring my vision. I don't know if I can make it the fifteen minutes it takes to pull into my driveway. I pull off to the side of the road and put my car in park. Luckily I'm in an area that doesn't see a lot of traffic.

I lay my head on the steering wheel and let the sobs take over. I don't even know why I'm crying so hard. I went into that conversation prepared to not let Jake get to me, and just that one ounce of effort on his part has my walls splintering. How do I go from being so immensely happy that Reaf is everything I should be looking for in a guy to wondering if it's all a huge mistake?

I really wish I had asked Cami to go with me to mediate and not let me turn into an emotional mess. Damn baby hormones. I wonder if Cami went back to sleep after I text her, or if by some miracle she's still awake. I'm hoping to talk her into coming over earlier than expected.

Picking up my phone, I try to reign in the tears, and dial my best friend.

"Hey, Chica," she answers.

"Cami? Do you think you could come over sooner rather than later?" I ask.

"Oh no, you have your crying voice. What happened? I'll be there in ten," she replies.

"I'll explain when you get to the house. I'm parked on the side of the road right now, but we should get there around the same time." I'm still trying to keep the tremble out of my voice, but it's obviously not working.

Cami sighs, and I know she feels for me. "Okay, be careful and if you're not there when I get there, I'll wait a few minutes before sending out a search party."

I can't help but laugh. Leave it to Cami to get me to laugh when I'm drowning in the saltiness of my own tears. "Ok, see you in a few."

I hang up and go to put my phone in the cup holder when I see a text from Reaf flash across the screen. I can't talk to him right now. I drop my phone in the holder, put my car in drive and head home so Cami can throw some wisdom at me.

I pull into my driveway just as Cami turns onto my street. She's got freaky timing. But I don't know what I would do without her. She's always there to have my back, and right now I couldn't be more grateful. I need to pull myself together so I can have a reasonable conversation without word vomiting everywhere. I'm not sure how this is going to go, but Cami will help me sort everything out. I still haven't responded to Reaf, and I'm not sure how he's going to take that.

I'm reaching for the door handle when it's jerked out from under my hand. Cami is there to scoop me into a giant hug. That is her only downfall. I don't think she realizes she's squishing me, and this round thing protruding from my torso is a little uncomfortable.

"Um, do you think you can let me go?" I ask as I try to disentangle myself from her arms. Finally free, I let out a sigh. I never realized just how much of a grip Cami has, if I ever need a bodyguard she's at the top of my list.

"Sorry, I kind of forgot that you're carrying around a little more. Did I hurt the baby?" She looks like someone just stole her puppy. I let her freak out for just a minute before laughing and shaking my head.

"No worries, girl. Little Bean is just fine. Me, however, I may have a few bruises from that bone crushing grip. Have you been working out?"

She ignores my question, grabs my hand, and leads me to the house. She doesn't even bother asking me for my house key. She has her copy in the lock before I can even reach for my bag. After walking inside, she leads me to the living room, and orders me to sit on the couch. A few minutes later she's back with the tea kettle, one of my favorite mugs, and honey vanilla chamomile tea. My favorite.

As soon as Cami has everything situated, she turns to me, clasps her hands together, and asks, "So what happened?"

I start going into the story about how he wants to make things right between us, and be together to raise our child.

And how he was being incredibly sweet, and even bought my favorite coffee, even though I couldn't drink it. By the time I get to the part about me walking out of Brew's Clues, I'm sobbing and running my hands through my hair. "I just don't know what to do. I mean, he is the father of my baby, and he was my first love. But then there's Reaf. I can't just leave him hanging. He seems to actually care about me."

I can practically see all the words Cami has been holding in to let me finish my diatribe. It's like they've bubbled up in her mouth waiting for the dam to break.

She pulls my hands down from where they are pulling on the ends of my hair. "Well, I can't really tell you what to do, but you do realize that you don't have to be with Jake just because y'all are having a baby together right? Hell, you don't even have to let him be a part of your life if you don't want to. But I don't suggest that. So, here's what I would do... Call Reaf, let him know what's going on. He seems like he might be a standup guy, and would understand. Or, at least listen to how your feeling. I can tell you have feelings for him. I haven't seen this happiness glow on you in forever, and you shouldn't waste it on confusion."

I start to object, but Cami puts her hand over my mouth. "I don't want to hear all the excuses. I know you're scared. I would be, too. This is just something you're going to have to figure out, little by little. And it's only fair to let Reaf know how you're handling all of it. I'm going to go get us some food, and while I'm gone you need to call Reaf. Don't think I won't check your phone when I get back. What does Little Bean want?"

Sighing, I answer. "How about Mexican food? I could really go for some menudo right about now." That comment was totally worth the face that Cami is making right now. I know she hates the stuff, but it's my comfort food, and she offered. Pregnant lady wins, always.

Cami grabs her keys, and as soon as I hear the door close, I sink into the sofa. How do I even go about having this conversation with Reaf. He doesn't need to deal with all the drama it appears my life is becoming right now. But he also needs to know that I care about him.

I pick up my phone from the table. Apparently, Cami put it there with her ninja like moves. My heart warms at the thought of her looking out for me. Grasping the phone in both hands, I take a deep breath. I look for Reaf's name in my contacts and press the button to call him. And I wait for him to answer.

twenty

IT DOESN'T TAKE LONG for me to wait. Reaf has already answered by the second ring. My hands are clammy and I'm starting to sweat. What is it about this guy that makes me lose my mind? I've never been shy a day in my life, but he seems to bring out the timid girl in me.

"Hello?" He asks, like this isn't the first time he's said it. "Tonya, are you there?"

"Oh, yeah. Sorry." I say, breathless. "I guess I kind of zoned out for a bit. I need to talk to you about something. It's not exactly bad, but I feel like this is something I should discuss with you since you've become an important part of my life."

I hear him take a deep breath. I can only imagine what he has going through his head right now. None of it good, most likely. "Okay," Reaf whispers.

"I met Jake for coffee earlier this morning. And he wants to be a part of the baby's life, but he also mentioned getting back together. I care about you, a lot. But... I'm confused as hell right now. I don't know where to go with him being a part of Little Bean's life. I mean he's at a university that isn't anywhere near here, and I ended things with him because he was an ass."

I'm twirling my hair through my fingers, a nervous habit I've had since I was little, when I hear Reaf sigh. His voice is just a whisper, "Are you breaking up with me? I mean, I understand, but it's not what I want. And I feel like maybe it's not what you want either."

I'm shaking my head, even though I know he can't see me. "No, I'm not breaking up with you. I just wanted to let you know what was happening. I may be confused, but I do want to see where things are going with us. You've kind of attached yourself to me. It may be a little soon, but I don't care. I like you, a whole hell of a lot."

I know he's smiling when he says, "Okay, good. What are you doing today? Want some company?"

I can't help the massive grin taking over my features. Like I said, this guy makes me feel different. And with just his reassurances, I know I've made the right choice in seeing what this is between Reaf and I.

"Actually, Cami just went to go get me and her some lunch. I can ask her if she's up for you coming over. She has been dying to meet you, after all."

"Sounds good, just let me know what she says. I'll talk to you later T. Bye."

As soon as he hangs up I click the speed dial for Cami. "Hey weirdo, you up for some company? Reaf wants to come over and this is the perfect opportunity for you to meet him."

I know she can't resist the temptation of peppering Reaf

with questions. "Sure," She replies. "Ask him if he wants anything before I order, and I'll grab it."

"You got it. I'll text you in a bit." I rush before hanging up the phone.

I text Reaf before he misses his opportunity for food.

> **Me:** Cami says it's cool if you hang with us. Want any food? She's getting Mexican.
> **Reaf:** Sure, a couple of tacos.
> **Me:** Okie dokie. I'll see you in a bit.

Time to let Cami know before she makes it out of the restaurant.

> **Me:** He wants a couple of tacos. He didn't specify so surprise him.
> **Cami:** Sure thing, captain. At the counter now. I'm really excited to interrogate my latest victim.

I chuckle, and wait for my best friend, and my boyfriend to spend the day with me. Nothing could be better.

* * *

I honestly don't know how I got so lucky to have such an amazing best friend and a guy that cares about how I'm feeling. I know if the roles were reversed, Jake would not be as chill with all my emotions as Reaf is being. Sometimes I fear he is *too* perfect, but I'm not one to look a gift horse in the mouth.

We started yet another Harry Potter marathon. Yes, I've

seen it a million times. No, I don't care that it makes me a huge nerd. The interrogation didn't last too long. Cami said we weren't eating until she was sure he was an okay guy. I'm pretty sure she knows he is, but she's gotta put her ninja bestie suit on for a bit.

I swear she is as bad as my dad. I think Reaf may be a bit terrified of her now. But after grilling him about his job, family, and why he was wanting to get with a preggo chick, she deemed him worthy of dating me. Not that I needed her approval, but it definitely helps to have her on my side.

I'm sandwiched between the both of them as the third movie starts up. I've been granted popcorn holding status. Beware those that try to snatch this buttery goodness out of my hands. You'll likely get throat punched. Reaf starts to put his arm around me, but thinks better of it since Cami is literally right next to me. And that would be weird. Although, it's slightly weird that she's so close to me. Maybe it's her way of marking her territory, and letting Reaf know that she was here first.

As I'm watching, I realize that this is something Jake would never do. He never understood all my nerdy awesomeness, and he never really got along with Cami. The thought of him sours my mood. I grab the remote and turn the volume down a bit. When I lean back into the sofa cushions, both Reaf and Cami are staring at me.

Cami peers around me at Reaf. "That is her 'she wants to talk but can't get her words arranged' face." She looks at me. "Spill."

I sigh. She knows me all too well. "I was just thinking that it's completely ridiculous for me to even consider any emotions for Jake because I'm pregnant. This, right here, watching amazing wizardry, is something he would have never done with us before."

I turn my gaze to Reaf. "You have no idea how much this moment means to me. You aren't trying to pull me away from my friend. You're willing, and enjoying, hanging out with both of us."

He opens his mouth to say something, but I cut him off. "Thank you for sticking with me, even when my emotions are all out of whack. And for reminding me what I should be focused on."

I put my arms around him, and hug him as well as I can with this big belly in the way, and the awkward angle. Reaf whispers in my ear, "You don't have to thank me for that. I'm here as long as you'll have me. I wish you could see yourself through my eyes."

I'm pretty sure my face is a beautiful shade of red right now. I can feel the tips of my ears burning. I sit back, ready to resume the movie. "You know, Christmas is next week. I want both of y'all to spend it here with me. I know you've got your own family things going on, but let me know what time works for y'all."

Cami squeals. "You bet your sweet ass I'll be here. We usually do our thing in the morning, but I can be here as soon as that mess is over with. I was actually trying to figure out a plan to get out of there as soon as possible."

I grin. "You know you can come here anytime you want, right? You have a fudging key for a reason. Use it."

Cami scrunches up her nose. "Did you just say 'fudging'?"

Sighing, I nod. "Yep, Dad thinks I need to cut back on my colorful language."

"Do I get key access, too?" Reaf asks.

"Only if you want my dad to castrate you," I respond.

"I'm going to go with no on that. But since Cami can't come until Christmas afternoon, and we usually do celebratory things in the morning, want to spend Christmas morning with my family?" Reaf asks, eagerly.

I'm stunned. I honestly didn't think he'd ask, but before the words can even leave my mouth, I nod. He has a schoolboy grin, and leans back. "Let's get on with this marathon."

I lean back, and snuggle into Reaf. When I tell Little Bean how I started to fall in real love for the first time, it'll be this moment. With Reaf and Cami surrounding me with hope, and glimpses into what my future could be.

twenty-one

LAST NIGHT WAS PERFECT. It's those moments that make me realize that what I had with Jake wasn't real. And I know what I have to do now. I need to make everything perfectly clear with him. I can't let him think there will be anything more than being parents to this little person growing inside me. I saw the hope in his eyes yesterday that there would be something more, and that just isn't possible. I won't allow myself to be tied to someone I don't love just because we have a child together. He's not going to like hearing it, but he doesn't have much of a choice. I just hope he doesn't cause problems for me...or Reaf.

It's funny how these moments of clarity tend to happen when I'm lazing about in bed. I roll onto my back and blow out a breath. This isn't going to be a pleasant conversation, and I feel like I might need my parents around to have my back in case Jake gets a little loud. And the fact that I know that's a possibility just goes to show that I don't need to be with him. I shouldn't fear his outbursts when I do or say something he doesn't agree with.

Scooting to the edge of the bed I grab my phone. I need to see if the parents are awake so we can set up a time to talk to Jake. I don't want to put this confrontation off for longer than I have to. I walk through the silent hall to the kitchen. I can already smell the bacon permeating the air. I swear my parents spoil me. They think that just because I'm pregnant I need to be fed constantly. At this rate I'll never lose the baby weight once this kid is born.

"Good morning parental units," I exclaim as I snatch a piece of bacon off the plate on the counter. I have to be quick because Mom is not a fan of me grabbing food off the plate before everyone is ready to eat. Luckily her back is turned. After eating my piece of bacon I say, "We need to talk."

Mom turns around. "Nothing good ever follows those words. What's up hon?"

"Well my little chat with Jake yesterday was a huge disaster." I give her all the details as she wraps me in her arms. "After spending time with Cami and Reaf yesterday afternoon I know what I need to do, and I need you there when I do it. I'm going to let Jake know once and for all that I'm not going to have a romantic relationship with him. And since he has a habit of going off the deep end when he's pissed, I want you or Dad, maybe both of you, there when I tell him. I figure the best way to accomplish that is if we invite him over here so that we can tell him to leave if need be."

Mom's nodding her head. "Absolutely, when do you want to do it?"

"I'd like to do it today if we can. I don't want to put it off.

It's not fair to me or Reaf to let Jake think he has a chance to be with me." I fiddle with the napkins that are next to the bacon. "Can we do it?

"Sure," Mom says. "Your dad should be home soon. How does lunch sound? Do you think he'd be able to come chat on such short notice?"

"Yep. I think he'll do just about anything right now. I don't think I'm going to tell him what this talk is about until he gets here. I don't want to give him the opportunity to bail, or come up with pretty words to try to sway my opinion."

Mom is pulling plates down from the counter. She places them on the counter. Since Dad isn't here right now, we tend to keep it simple. There's no reason to use the massive table when it's just the two of us. As she sits down she tells me to text him.

Me: *Can you come over for lunch?*
Jake: *Sure. I'll be there around 12:30.*

I grab my fork ready to take my first bite. "He'll be here after 12. Now we wait and prepare for the shit storm that's bound to happen."

Mom just nods in agreement.

* * *

There's a knock on the door, and I know my time is up. I have to face this head on. I can't let him try to sweet talk and charm his way back into my life.

I open the door and see the smug smirk on Jake's face.

131

It's a good thing I asked my parents to hang around the house today in case I need them for back up.

"Are you going to come in?" I gesture toward the living room, and Jake stands there for a second longer before he steps over the threshold.

"I'm glad you let me come over today so we can talk," he says as he sits on the couch. He takes the middle seat so that I have no choice but to sit beside him. Ugh, will his stupid games never end?

"You didn't give me much of a choice, but we do need to talk." I sigh while twisting my hands in my lap.

He places a hand over mine, and uses his other hand to tilt my face up. I'm looking into his eyes now, and I can't help but remember how sweet he can be when he actually tries to be.

"Please, take me back. I know I said it yesterday, but I mean it. Don't you think this is what's right? This baby needs both of us, and together we are a united front."

I'm already shaking my head. "No, I don't want to get back with you. We can be united parents without having to be together. You've got great things going for you. And, honestly, I don't want to be with you. I think we can do this separately. Besides, I'm seeing someone. I'm not going to drop him because you think us having a child will end in some kind of happily ever after. That's not how it works."

"Dammit, Tonya. What do I have to do to prove to you that I'm different? That I want to be the man you need." He stands abruptly.

"There's nothing you can do. There will always be a part of me that cares about you, but I can't chance my happiness on hoping things will be different. I've moved on. And if you were serious about us, you would have made this stand a long time ago."

I know I didn't give him much a chance since I practically shoved him out the door when I told him. But he's doing this for all the wrong reasons, and I don't know how to get him to understand that.

"You're right, I didn't. But this is what needs to happen. Do you have any idea the crap I've been getting from my parents because I didn't even know I was going to be a father?"

I knew it. "So this is all so you can look better for your parents? That's definitely not a good reason for me to take you back. It will all end in a disaster.

"That's not the only reason, Tonya." Jake sighs, and shakes his head. "You're the only girl I've ever loved. How am I supposed to feel knowing that you are carrying my child but with someone else? It's hard."

"Look Jake, I know it will be weird for a while, but we can get through all this. Reaf is a great guy. He's been there for me when I didn't think I had anyone that could relate. I'm not going to dump him to take you back. And if all we're going to do is argue that point, then I think it's best that you leave." I slowly pull myself from the couch, and walk slowly toward the front door. I'm stressed, and exhausted, and need a nap.

"Fine, but this isn't over. I will prove to you that we're good together. That we can make a relationship and family work." He stalks out the front door.

"It's not worth the effort, Jake. When you want to talk about co-parenting, come see me. Until then... please, just stay away."

When I close the door, I can hear his back tires screeching as he peals out of my driveway. I'm happy I didn't need Mom to help me stand up for myself. But Jake is persistent, he meant what he said. I just hope he keeps his antics to driving me crazy and doesn't do anything to Reaf.

twenty-two

MOM HAD no problem moving our Christmas celebration so that Cami and Reaf could be here with us. She's even making tamales for it. I swear, I have the best mom in the world. It's no easy task, so I'm helping her put each one together.

It's Christmas Eve, and we have *The Grinch* playing on the TV for background noise. I love the movie version better than the cartoon. Jim Carey does a fabulous job portraying the mean spirited Who that has a change of heart.

After we have the last tamale put together and the kitchen is cleaned up, Mom and I sit in the living room with rolls of wrapping paper surrounding us. I love that she gets the cutesy wrapping paper. I don't think I'll ever outgrow the fun gift wrap of my youth.

"Mom, I'm nervous," I whisper as I'm wrapping the tie I bought for Dad.

"Sweetheart, there's nothing to be worried about. You did a pretty good job of facing down Jake last weekend. Meeting Reaf's family is going to a piece of cake. You've already met his nephew. And his brother goes to the high school you just graduated from. Now you just have to meet his sister and mother. If she raised such a gentleman, I have no doubt that she'll love you." Mom says while placing a hand on my shoulder.

"But what if she takes one look at my massive belly, and thinks I'm just looking for someone to take care of my baby."

"She won't. But if she does, I know you'll win her over quickly. You're a beautiful young woman, Mija. I just wish you could see what the rest of us do." She rubs my back, and then continues shuffling paper around until she finds the one she wants to use.

"If you say so, Ma. I'm just ready for tomorrow to be here so I can get through all the awkward feelings." I push Dad's wrapped gift under the massive tree taking up residence in our living room.

The lights are on, and they twinkle in the best way possible. Looking at the tree, I feel hope that maybe everything will be okay. My Christmas wish is to have a wonderful day with family and friends.

* * *

I'm lying in bed, still slightly freaking out about meeting Reaf's family tomorrow. I'm just about to put my book down when I hear my phone vibrate on the nightstand beside my bed. The room is so quiet, I jump at the noise.

Reaf: Are you up?
Me: Yup. Why are you still awake?

Instead of getting a reply, my phone starts buzzing in my hand.

I swipe the screen to answer the phone. "Why are you calling me, weirdo?"

Hearing Reaf's chuckle through the receiver sets off a wave of butterflies in my stomach.

"Weirdo? Is that how you always answer the phone?"

"Not usually, but since I knew it was you, I figured I'd try it out."

"So, why are you still awake," he asks.

I'm twirling my hair around my finger as I respond. "Just having a minor panic attack about meeting your family. No big deal."

"Don't worry, they're going to love you."

I sigh. "I hope you're right. It would really suck if they don't."

"Try to get some sleep. I'll come pick you up in the morning so you don't have to drive. You can even take a tiny cat nap on the way, since I have a feeling you're going to be exhausted."

I giggle. "It's not my fault, worry makes me lose sleep. And I don't nap that much."

"Oh yes, you do. It seems like anytime I call or text, you're just waking up or trying to go back to sleep."

"Okay, fine. So I sleep a lot. You try being huge and tired all the time."

"I'm good. But thanks. Go to sleep gorgeous. I'll see you bright and early."

I can already feel my eyelids starting to droop. His reassuring voice quelling my anxiety.

"Goodnight, Reaf. I'll see you in the morning."

"Night, Beautiful," are the last words I hear before giving way to slumber.

* * *

Reaf just text me to let me know he's on his way. I'm beyond nervous, but I need to do my best not to show it. I don't want him to spend the entire time trying to keep me calm. I'm a big girl. I can handle it... I think.

Before long I hear a knock at the front door. My parents are awake because they are always up early on Christmas morning. It feels a little weird not being in the living room opening presents as a family, but I'm happy Mom and Dad were okay with everything being shifted. I think they realize how much Reaf means to me. But they also know I will do pretty much anything to spend extra time with Cami. These past few months have been hell without her.

I walk slowly into the living room where Reaf and my parents are waiting. I plaster on a smile, and hope I am showing more confidence than I feel.

Reaf is standing there, between my parents, with a wide smile on his face. "You look beautiful."

I can feel my cheeks reddening. I try to look at the ground, but my belly makes that a little difficult. "Thank you. You're not so bad yourself."

Seconds later his thumb and forefinger are lifting my chin up. "Look at me."

I stare into his eyes. They are so bright and full of hope. They are my guiding light into what I hope is a possible future. It's refreshing being in a relationship and excited to see the person you're with. When you're not scared of what you're going to do next to piss them off.

He's looking at me like I'm the most precious thing in the world. "You are stunning, kind and caring. I wish you could see yourself through my eyes."

I smile. I can't help it. He says all the right things and knows how to calm my nerves. And, he just said all that in front of my parents. He isn't scared to let the world know how he feels about me.

I stroll over to Mom and Dad, give them a hug and kiss on the cheek, then grab Reaf's hand and lead him toward the door.

I'm shocked to see that his car is still running. He constantly amazes me by doing all the small things. As I slide into the passenger seat, I shed my jacket and bask in the warmth blowing from the vents.

Fifteen minutes later we're pulling into his driveway. I'm twisting my hands around themselves until Reaf places a hand over them. He grabs my left hand and places a quick kiss along my knuckles.

"You ready," he asks while interlocking his fingers with mine.

I nod. I feel like I can do anything with him standing by my side.

Reaf opens the door, and we briskly walk up the porch steps and into the house. I'm immediately bombarded by David. He wraps his small arms around my leg and holds tight.

"You came back to see me," he squeals.

"I sure did, little buddy," I reply while I ruffle his hair.

I hear a sweet voice call out. "David don't maul our guest."

We turn the corner into the living room and there stands a brown-eyed woman slightly older than Reaf and I. There's a slight family resemblance in the way their faces are shaped, but they couldn't be more different.

She puts out a hand to shake mine. "I'm Caroline. And you must be Tonya. I've heard so much about you."

I blush. I seem to be doing that a lot today. "Yes, it's nice to meet you."

Caroline is quickly pushed aside, and I'm being embraced by another woman. She's about my height, and exudes warmth and all happy things.

She's talking so fast I can barely understand her. "I'm sooo happy to *finally* meet you. I was hoping to catch a glimpse of you the one night Reaf brought you over, but y'all managed to evade me."

I laugh, "You must be Maggie. Reaf has said wonderful things about you."

Maggie snorts. "He better have. Now, where's Bryce so we can get the introductions out of the way."

We all walk out of the living room, cross the hall, and step into the kitchen. That is where we find Bryce. He's trying to grab a handful of bacon off the plate on the dining table, when Maggie slaps his hand and he drops it.

I murmur to Reaf. "I see she has the same quick slap that my mom does."

He chuckles and shakes his head. "Hey Bryce, this is Tonya."

Bryce just gives me a small head nod acknowledging my

presence in the way young teens want you to think they are cool.

Maggie claps her hands together. "Everyone take a seat. I hope you're hungry Tonya."

"Absolutely. I'm hungry all the time." I say, smiling.

The round dining room table is loaded with food, and there's not a visible spot on it except for the edges where there are plates already set. I sit there waiting to see who is going to start passing each dish, but everyone just starts digging into what they want. I could get down with this way of dining. I pick up my plate and load it up with bacon, French toast, eggs, and a blueberry muffin that is so massive it may topple off.

Everyone is busy eating, so conversation is light. I learn that they moved here not too long ago, which explains why Reaf didn't go to school with me.

Maggie explains, "When we found out that Caroline and David were going to be moving in with us, we needed a slightly bigger house. I forgot how much room little ones need, especially with the amount of toys they accumulate."

I gape in horror. "You mean their stuff spreads out of their own room?"

Caroline is laughing. "You'll see for yourself soon. But even with the mess, I wouldn't have it any other way. When days seem exceptionally awful, David's bright eyes make everything seem better."

I can't help but smile. The love she has for her child is apparent, and I have a feeling I'll feel the same way once Little Bean is here.

Everyone is finally done eating, and honestly, there isn't much food left. I thought there'd be a ton of food still sitting on the table. Apparently everyone brought their appetite this morning. I start gathering plates so I can help with clean up, but Reaf quickly grabs the plates out of my hand and places them back on the table.

"You don't need to worry about that. Bryce and I will get all this cleaned up after presents. I think David might explode if we put it off any longer." Reaf says putting his arm around my shoulder. I sink into him, loving the comfort and support.

"Okay, I just wanted to help." I whisper.

"You don't have to do a thing." Reaf leads me to a huge recliner beside the fireplace. I sink into it. It has got to be the most comfortable thing I've ever sat in. It's plush and I feel like I'm being snuggled. I need one of these at the house. I could fall asleep in it with zero problems.

Reaf sits on the floor beside me. He could probably fit in this chair with me, but I appreciate the fact that he's letting me have such a roomy place to relax. I run my fingers back and forth through his hair and can feel his body relax. He must have been just as nervous as I was. All that panic I put myself through before wasn't needed. His family is welcoming and they haven't once made any comments about him dating me while I'm pregnant with someone else's child. I wonder if they know how beyond grateful I am for that.

Maggie and Caroline are sitting on the sofa, Bryce is on the floor in front of their Christmas tree, and David is jumping up and down. Ready to tear into the wrapping paper.

Bryce begins making piles for each person, and I'm a little shocked when there's a tiny pile for me. Then I feel awful because I didn't bring anything. That just means I'll have to go shopping this coming up weekend. After meeting them, I have ideas for what would be perfect for them.

David doesn't let the pile grow too much before he is ripping paper off of boxes. I see his triumphant smile when he shows off a giant firetruck that makes all kinds of noises. I'm not really paying attention to what anyone else is opening. But the stack beside Reaf has various art supplies.

I finally get the courage to open the gifts for me. One is a cute beanie in hot pink and gray. The other is a large square. I open it up and see a leather bound scrapbook. The front is engraved with "Little Bean's First Year," and I can't keep the tears from springing up in my eyes. It's something so small, but yet so impactful.

Maggie speaks up. "I made you the beanie after Reaf told me what your favorite colors are. But he also told us you refer to the baby as Little Bean. Caroline and I wanted to do something special for you."

I jump out of the recliner and rush Maggie and Caroline. I didn't know I could move so fast, but soon I have both of them in my arms and my body is shaking with my sobs. Now I know where Reaf gets his kind demeanor from. He has two amazing examples under the same roof.

"Thank you so much," I say between breaths. "You have no idea how much this means to me."

We have a weird sort of group hug going on, so it takes a bit to disentangle ourselves from each other. Maggie wipes the tears from my face, and gives me a soft peck on my cheek.

"You're very welcome. Just promise you'll come around. You're welcome any time."

"I will," I promise. And I know it's true because I don't think there's anything that could make me turn away from this new relationship.

Reaf walks up behind and wraps his arms around my waist. His hands resting on my growing baby bump.

"Are you ready to head back to your place," he whispers in my ear. "I'm sure Cami is ready to get out of her house."

I nod. "Yeah, I'm ready. Are you ready for the crazy amounts of food my mom has probably prepared?"

"Absolutely. As long as I can sneak in a nap at some point."

I giggle. "Now you're starting to sound like me."

He grins and leads me to the door. But before we walk out, he turns back. I see him put a small wrapped box in his pocket. Now, I can't wait until we get to the house. I want to know what's in that box.

twenty-three

THE DRIVE back to the house flies by. My hand is interlocked with Reaf's, and it is utter perfection. He has the radio turned to the local alternative station, and I'm completely lost in the music. Wondering how I got so lucky to have such a supportive group of people surrounding me.

That euphoric feeling goes away as we start to slow, and Reaf's grip on my hand increases. I look up and see fucking Jake parked in front of my house.

Reaf tries to mask the anger in his voice. "What is he doing here?"

"I don't know," I reply shaking my head. "I told him not to come back unless he was ready to talk about co-parenting and not about us getting back together. Maybe that's what he wants."

This really isn't the best day to be hashing this shit out. And I'm not amused. Reaf parks the car.

"I'll be right back. I'm going to deal with this and then we're going to have an amazing rest of the day." I say pulling my hand from his.

"Nope. That's not happening. I think the only way he's going to get the message is if I'm with you, and we show him that we're a united front."

I start to argue, and get a little pissed that this may be a pissing contest when he cuts in. "Before you get that adorable frown on your face, this isn't a jealousy thing. If he's willing to be a part of Little Bean's life, and be respectful of your relationships, then I'm all for getting along with him. I just don't want him to think he can make you push me aside."

I sigh. "I guess... Just don't get all territorial and caveman."

All he does is grin and get out of the car before coming to the passenger side and opening the door for me. He grabs my hand, and we turn to face Jake. I don't miss how he stands a little in front of me like he's my own personal shield. So much for not acting like a caveman. At least he's subtle about it.

I glance at Jake. "What do you want Jake?" I hope he can hear how tired I am of all this back and forth.

He looks between Reaf and I. "Can I talk to you alone?"

"Nope. Whatever you need to say, you can say it in front of Reaf. He's not going anywhere." I say while shaking my head.

Jake glares at Reaf. It must really bug him that I won't talk to him alone, but I don't have anything else to say.

"I still think we should get back together. Let me prove to you how great we could be." Jake grounds out. I can see his teeth clenching while making this remark.

Sighing I say, "We've had this talk before, and you know

what my response is. Honestly, I'm kind of tired of going through the same thing over and over again."

"But, please, just give me a--," Jake starts.

I hold up my hand. "No. Now, I'd like you to leave, and if not, I'll go get my father and he can make you leave."

I know it's pretty shitty of me to resort to using my dad to take care of my problem, but I don't want Reaf put in an awkward position. And, this is their house, so I'm sure he'd be happy to make sure Jake leaves.

I can almost see Jake folding into himself. His shoulders slump and he turns around. He gets into his car, and just sits there for a minute before driving off. I expected him to peal out, and drive like a bat out of hell. But I think he got the point this time. He can't force me to be with him. I'm just wondering how long it will be before he tries to do the same crap again.

* * *

As we walk up the sidewalk, I see the blinds in the living room move just the slightest. They were watching the whole time. Why would they just not turn Jake away the minute he got here? Parents make no sense whatsoever.

Reaf opens the door and leads us inside. He's already comfortable enough with me and my family to walk in without having me open the door ahead of him. When we get to the living room, I come to a stop. Dad has a huge grin on his face, and is walking toward Reaf.

Dad pulls Reaf into a weird side hug. I'm standing there shocked. Just a few weeks ago, Dad was telling me how dating Reaf was a mistake, and now... Now he's acting like they are buddies. Maybe I've stepped into the *Twilight Zone*.

Dad pulls back and claps Reaf on the shoulder. "I appreciate you being my little girl's protector."

I stare at him dumbfounded. "He didn't even do anything. Why are you thanking him?"

Dad rolls his eyes. "I know you did all the talking, but the way this young man put himself in front of you was his way of showing Jake that he'd have to go through him before he got to you. That is what I respect."

I release a gush of air, and shake my head. I will never understand the male way of thinking. Although, it does warm my insides knowing that Dad is starting to get on board with this whole dating situation.

I turn to Mom, who just sat down in my favorite chair. "Have you heard from Cami? I figured she'd be here by now."

Mom shakes her head. "Nope, why don't you call her. Maybe she was waiting on you to give her the excuse she needs to leave the house. You know how her parents can be."

I wish there was a way Mom could adopt Cami, even though she's already an adult. I think we care more about her well-being than her own parents do. All they care about is how they look.

I walk into my room, and sit on the bed. The comforter is still askew since I forgot to make my bed this morning. That should clue you into how out of sorts I was about meeting Reaf's family. I *always* make my bed. Now that I'm comfortable, I call Cami.

She answers mid-ring. "Please tell me you are home."

I laugh. I can't help it. "Yes, dork. I'm home. You heading over."

I hear the desperation in her voice. "Hell yes. I need out of this hell-hole. I'll be there in a few."

She doesn't even say bye, just hangs up. They must be on her ass more than usual. I take off my shoes in favor of my super comfortable slipper socks. I'm at home now, and don't really have to impress anyone. Besides... comfort is more important.

By the time I make it back into the living room, I can hear Cami's car pull into the driveway. Mom must be in the kitchen heating up the tamales. I cannot wait to dig into that bit of yumminess. I haven't had tamales in forever. I remember helping my great-grandmother make them every year when I was a kid. As she got older, it turned into only getting tamales on your birthday. I miss those times. I really need to go see her soon. Maybe after Little Bean is born Cami and I can make the trip.

Cami rushes at me as soon as she walks through the front door. There's no time for me to brace myself before she has her arms around me and her face in my neck. I'm kind of at a loss at what I'm supposed to do. I look at Reaf, and he can see that I need help.

He answers my silent plea. "Hey Cami, how's it going?"

With that Cami straightens up and masks whatever emotion was overwhelming her when she barged into the house.

She shrugs. "Same old, same old. Asshole parents, ridiculous expectations, but I'm here now, so it's better."

I grab Cami's hand and give it a quick squeeze. "We'll talk about it later," I whisper. She only nods.

The three of us go to the kitchen to see if Mom needs any help. And by help, I mean help sampling the food until it's time to eat. I know, I know, I just ate not that long ago... But this mama is hungry. The smells surrounding the kitchen makes my stomach grumble. We would typically have tamales, Spanish rice, and beans on Christmas Eve, and a traditional Christmas dinner on Christmas day. But I wanted to share all the amazing food with my friends, so last night we had soup so that today could be special.

I'm pretty sure I just heard Reaf's stomach growl too.

I look over my shoulder at him. "Have you ever had homemade Mexican food?"

"Does the food at restaurants count?" He asks.

"Sometimes, but usually... no. It tastes better when you know you've made it." I pull a tortilla out of the tortilla warmer, and pull the butter out of the fridge. After spreading a sensible layer of butter on the warm tortilla, I hand it to Reaf.

"This is the best way to eat a tortilla. Eat this and then tell me you think restaurant Mexican food is the same as homemade." I know he can't. It's one of the reason it's hard for me to find a Mexican restaurant I like, I'm too damn picky. If it tastes slightly processed, I'm out.

Reaf moans after taking the first bite, and then quickly gobbles up the rest of it. He looks around, sheepish. Cami is laughing at his reaction.

"Don't be embarrassed," she says. "I had pretty much the same reaction."

Reaf turns to me and with fake seriousness says, "Marry me."

I laugh so hard I'm doubling over. It's one of the laughs

you can feel throughout your entire body. "Thanks for the offer, but no. I'm good. But I told you homemade is the best."

I'm about to grab another tortilla when Mom snatches the container out of my hands.

"What the crap? I'm hungry... Why did you do that?"

Mom just looks at me like I know better, and I do, but that doesn't keep me from pouting. "No more tortillas. You'll ruin your appetite," She admonishes.

"But I didn't even get to have one," I whine, glaring at Cami and Reaf. They both ate one, but I can't. This is totally not fair.

Luckily, I don't have to wait long until we eat. Mom has the food spread out on the bar so that we can all sit at the table without the massive amounts of food taking up space. There is absolutely no conversation happening. Everyone is busy shoveling food in their mouths. I'm already on my second helping as everyone is finishing their first round. I always take advantage when Mom puts together a dinner like this one since we rarely eat tamales. They are just too time consuming to make all the time.

Soon everyone is finished eating, and now I'm miserable. I ate entirely too much, and I have no idea how I'm going to move. But I don't have to worry about that. Reaf gets out of his chair and extends his hand to me. With more grace than I expected to have he helps me out of my seat. He has his arm around my waist leading me to the living room, and my favorite chair before Mom tries to steal it again. I can hear Cami making gagging noises behind us. That's okay, though. Just wait until she finds someone that makes her heart beat double time.

Once we are all situated, Mom looks at Dad. "You are Santa tonight. You even have the gray hairs to match."

Dad scoffs, "So then, why exactly are there always boxes of hair dye in the trashcan?" Then he winks at her.

I love that they banter like this. She has a spark in her eyes when she gazes at my dad, and you can see just how much they adore each other. Usually I'm disgusted by their playful demeanor, but tonight... It makes me happy, and thankful that I have parents that are still ridiculously in love with each other.

Reaf is on the floor in front of me, just like he was at his house. Cami is lying across the couch, while Mom and Dad are sitting on the floor in front of the Christmas tree. Dad starts handing out the gifts.

Even Reaf has a small pile in front of him. I thought I was the only one who got him something, but apparently my parents did as well. Mom counts down from three, and we all being tearing the paper off.

Mom and Dad got me clothes I can wear after I have the baby. Courtesy of Mom. I don't think Dad even knows what type of clothes I like. They basically consist of plain tops, yoga pants, and of course t-shirts that display some of my favorite fandoms. There are also a few gift cards to various stores. Cami is busy smelling all the body lotions and candles I bought her. They bought Reaf some gift cards. I'm sure they didn't know what to get him. He opens the gift I bought him, and acts like it's the best gift ever. They are a pair of *Harry Potter* headphones. If he's going to date me... He needs to bask in the nerdiness.

He slips the box he had in his pocket into my lap. I quickly unwrap and open the jewelry box. It's a necklace with a black heart, and the back has an engraving that says *follow your heart*. I swear, this boy makes me swoon so hard.

"I wasn't sure what to get you, but I saw this necklace and knew it was perfect for you. I had them engrave the message. I just wanted to make sure you knew you could follow your heart, no matter where it may lead you." He has a small smile on his face, like he wasn't sure how I was going to respond.

I attempt to throw my arms around him, and almost fall. I forget how much this belly gets in the way sometimes. I scoot out of the chair so that I'm on the floor with him, and try again.

"I love it," I whisper into his ear. "Thank you, it's perfect."

Mom and Dad are starting to clean up the mess, and I jump up remembering I still haven't given Mom her gift.

"Hold on, y'all don't move," I yell as a run as fast as I can to my room.

I go into my bathroom and pull the envelope out from under the tampon box, that I won't need for a few more months. I figured it was the perfect hiding spot, and Mom would never find it.

I have my hands holding the envelope behind my back while walking into the living room. Mom is sitting next to Dad, bewildered. I lower myself in front of them, and hand the envelope to Mom.

She raises her eyebrows and asks, "Is this what I think it is?"

"Yep. I know you've been dying to find out if you'll have a granddaughter or grandson, and I wanted everyone together to find out." I say with a huge smile on my face. "Go on... Open it."

Her eyes are watery as she slowly opens the flap. I can feel the anticipation in the room. They all want to know what I'm having and the wait is torture for them. I'll be happy either way... As long as Little Bean is healthy.

Finally, Mom pulls out the ultrasound that will tell her boy or girl. She puts her hand to her mouth, and lets out a sob. I'm pretty sure it's a happy sob, but I can't really tell. What if the sex isn't on the ultrasound? What if it's a little message that says "sorry we couldn't determine at this time?"

Cami, ever impatient, runs behind Mom and grabs the ultrasound. Her eyes flick over the paper, and her eyes light up.

"OH MY GOSH! I get to buy all the pretty dresses," she squeals.

Well... It looks like I'm going to have a mini me running around.

twenty-four

WE SPENT the rest of the night watching Christmas movies and enjoying each other's company. Reaf went home around ten, and I was bummed he was leaving so soon. But I was getting tired.

Cami and I have just changed into our pajamas, and we're lying in bed. She's on Pinterest trying to find things to make sure my daughter will be camera ready at all times. I'm not exactly certain how she's going to ensure that since she'll be going back to school in a couple of weeks, but I'm not going to burst her bubble.

She's still scrolling when she asks, "Have you thought about names?"

I shake my head. "Not really. I'm still trying to process that I'm having a little girl."

"Don't worry about it yet. I'll help you pick out the perfect name for the Little Bean."

I laugh. "I'm not sure if that's comforting or terrifying. Just as long as it's not one of those off the wall names the celebrities are giving their kids."

Cami grins. "I can't make any promises."

I slap her arm. I have a feeling I'm going to be nixing a ton of the names she suggests. I roll on to my side so that I'm facing her.

"Okay girl, we need to talk," I say.

She groans. "Do we have to? I'm actually kind of tired."

She's deflecting, and she knows I'm on to her. I don't really want to end our night on heavy topics, but I need to figure out what's going on with my best friend. She's put on her happy face all day, but I can tell something is off. She has a darkness dimming her eyes, and I hate seeing it there.

"I don't think so. You're not getting out of this. What's going on? Why haven't you been answering my texts or calls as much as you used to?" I place my hand over hers.

Cami looks like she's about to burst into sobs. I can see tears streaming down her cheeks. I wrap my arm around her. It's the only way I know how to comfort her when I don't know what's wrong.

"I just feel so lost and unhappy. Dad has me on this fast track to become an accountant, and it's not what I want to do. I'm stressed and I have too much on my plate. I don't know what to do."

I'm patting her now like my parents used to do with me when I was upset. "I'm sorry, honey. Have you told your parents how you feel?"

"I tried to right before you called, but they wouldn't listen. They kept telling me that they know what is best for me. And that if I change my courses then they'll stop paying for school. I don't have a job or any kind of savings. How would I survive without their help?"

Cami is crying harder now, and I wish I could knock

some sense into her parents' heads. How can they not see that their daughter is falling apart? That she's not happy?

"Have you looked into scholarships," I ask. "If anything, you can get a part time job for the school and that usually brings tuition down. We'll figure something out. I can't stand to see you this upset because your parents are asshats."

She nods, and it seems like her crying has lessened. "Thank you for listening. And I'm sorry I've pulled away. I just didn't know how to deal with it all. Here you are, with your life turned upside down, still doing your best to better yourself. You're like my personal hero. I hope one day I can tackle the world like you do."

Chuckling I say, "It's not as easy as it looks. I've had my fair share of shitty days, and Jake being ridiculous doesn't help matters. I just hope after seeing me with Reaf today made him realize it's not going to happen between us."

Cami abruptly sits up. "Wait, you saw Jake today? When did this happen?"

"Actually, not long before I called you. He was waiting in the driveway when Reaf and I got here from his family's house."

"Well, what happened? How could you not mention that to me earlier?" Cami says, hurt tinging her words.

I fill her in on all the details, and everything that happened, especially how Reaf wouldn't let me face Jake alone. And how Jake left defeated.

She sighs dreamily, "Aw, that's so sweet. Reaf is your knight in shining armor. I'm pretty sure Jake knows that you're not going to back to him. There isn't anything he can do that can top the way Reaf has been there for you. And

Reaf didn't pressure you to date him. He won you over with his incredible sweetness and charm."

I try to find a comfortable position. "That he did. But do you think this is all going a little too fast with Reaf? We haven't been dating that long, and already I can't imagine not having him around. He makes my days brighter, and is constantly making me laugh."

Cami puts her hand on my forehead. "Are you sure you're not sick? I've never seen you so sappy about a relationship. But when you find someone you click with... You hang on to it. Don't let yourself become jaded like my parents. I want you to have a relationship like your parents. Having you, and them, in my life gives me hope that not all families are like mine. That I have a chance of finding my own happily ever after."

I think she's done with her speech, but she continues. "I see the way Reaf looks at you. Like you're the shining star in his sky. I want that." I start to laugh. "Don't laugh, you get that same gooey-eyed expression when you're around him. Whatever you do... Don't let that go."

"I won't," I promise her. It would take a lot for that to happen.

I turn off the lamp beside my bed and I'm about to close my eyes, when I feel something in my stomach. At first I think it's indigestion or something from the massive amounts of food I've eaten today, but it happens again. Harder. And there it is again.

I gasp, "Cami, feel. I think the baby's moving."

I pull her hand on my stomach in the area where I felt the first thump. I can tell when she feels it because she yanks her hand back.

"Oh my gosh, that feels weird and awesome at the same time," she says, excitement evident in the way her voice pitches higher.

"I know," I say. Happiness soaring. "I thought I had felt it before, but I wasn't sure. Now, I think Little Bean wants us to know she's listening."

We spend another hour waiting for the baby to kick again. Talking to her like she's already born. Telling her all the things we are going to do as she gets older.

I'm happy that my best friend is here to experience it with me, but I'm also a little sad that Reaf isn't here with us. Cami said it's possible for someone to feel this strongly for someone when they haven't been together long. But I'm starting to worry that I'm falling for him. Head over heels. And I'm not sure how I feel about that.

twenty-five

NEW YEAR'S Eve has always been a time I looked forward to. This year I'm feeling a little mellow. Jake, Cami, and I would see what small parties we could find and hang out until we brought the new year in together. But everything is different this year. I have a new, wonderful boyfriend, my best friend is going through a family crisis, and I'm knocked up. Don't get me wrong, I'm finally at a happy place with my pregnancy, but I kind of wish I was out. It's the one night I like to completely let loose and have fun.

I'm lying in my bed, covers piled on top of me because I can't seem to get warm, thinking about all the ways my life is going to change next year. I'll be starting my second semester of college, all online classes, and I'll have a tiny human I have to take care of. That terrifies me. I feel an anxiety attack coming on, and kick the mound of blankets off of me. What if I can't do this? What if I royally screw this kid up? My breaths are coming in quick pants, and I don't know how to stop them.

"Mom," I call out. Hoping she can quell this freak out.

My door flies open and Mom rushes in. "Is everything okay? Is it the baby? What's wrong?" I can hear the panic in her voice. I've never seen my mom afraid, but the look in her eyes show how scared she is that something may have happened to me or Little Bean.

"No, I just can't breathe." I say between gasps. "I'm kind of freaking out."

Mom climbs into the bed behind me, and starts running her fingers through my hair. I loved when she did this to me as a child. It's a small gesture that always brought me comfort. We stay like that for at least fifteen minutes before I feel like I've got my emotions back under control.

Still brushing my hair with her fingers Mom asks, "What is making you melt down?"

I take a deep breath and slowly let it out. "Life in general." I pause trying to gather my thoughts. "What if this is all too much for me? I'm scared I'm going to fuck everything up. And what if I can't manage school, work and a baby? I don't want to be that girl that mooches off her parents and can't take care of her own family."

Now that I've spewed all the words out, I feel a weight lift off my chest. I would have vented to Cami, but she wouldn't completely understand. I know she could tell me how to deal with the stress, but until she has had to face the decisions I have, she'll never truly get it. At least with Mom, she's had a child. She can see my point of view. And maybe... maybe she'll help lead me in the direction I need to go.

She laughs. Seriously, laughs. What the actual hell? She's not supposed to find my inner turmoil amusing. "Honey, you aren't feeling anything all new moms haven't felt. We all go through those freak out moments. I'm not going to lie and say it'll always be easy, but I have faith in you. You'll always do what you think is best. And you happen to have two pretty awesome parents to help you out when you need it. As long as you have a strong support system, you can do anything."

Part of me thinks everything she just said is one of those canned responses parents give their children to make them feel better. But the other part of me is happy to have such an amazing person behind me. Cheering me on.

"Thanks Mom." I roll over and give her an awkward hug. "That means a lot, and was kind of helpful. Well, except for the part where you laughed at me. That part sucked."

"Now," Mom says as she scoots off the bed. She makes her way around and grabs my arms. "You need to get up. I'll make you some breakfast, but before that I have a surprise for you."

I blink in confusion. "Surprise? What are you talking about?"

"You'll see." She winks at me and drags me out of bed.

We walk into the living room, and there are black and gold streamers covering every corner of the room. She even put some of those beaded gold strands over the doorways.

I'm in awe, but also a little confused. "What is all this?"

She beams. "I know you usually go out with Cami for New Year's Eve, and with you being pregnant I didn't think you'd want to do that this year. So, I brought the party to you. I invited Cami, Reaf, and his family. It's not going to be anything crazy, but I wanted to do something special for you."

I can barely keep my tears from flowing. "Thank you, Mom. This means a lot, and was part of what spurred my downward spiral into freak out zone."

"Anytime, sweetheart. Your dad even helped me put the streamers up." She says with pride lacing her words.

I start toward the kitchen because she promised me food. She's even decorated in here. There are more streamers, and she's placed champagne flutes on the bar. I can't help but be amazed at everything my parents do to make sure I have little sparkles of happiness in my life. I seriously don't know what I would do without them. I kind of want to make them a parents of the year award like I used to do when I was little.

The party is in full swing, and I'm happy I took a few catnaps today. There's no way I would have made it this late without them. Although, I think I've lost my best friend to my mom, Maggie, and Caroline. I'm pretty sure they are trying to plan a baby shower for me before Cami leaves for school again. They assume they're being sneaky, but this house is only so big.

Bryce looks like he'd rather be anywhere else but here. I feel bad that he got stuck coming here when he could be out with his friends. He's slouching on the couch, with the brim of his hat pulled over his face. He might actually be sleeping, though I don't see how. Mom has the music turned up pretty loud, and the TV is playing the New Year's Eve special.

At least David is occupied. We don't have any toys for him to play with so I brought my tablet out of the room. I downloaded a few games that are age appropriate. I'm not going to be the person that corrupts Caroline's child.

Reaf is sitting in my favorite chair, and I'm splayed across his lap. My head is on one arm of the chair, and my feet are dangling off the other side. I don't see how he isn't in pain from me being on top of him. But he keeps reassuring me that I'm not all that heavy. Proof that flattery will get you everywhere. He's lazily drawing circles on my arm with his finger. The touch is so soothing I almost fall asleep.

He gives my hair a gentle tug. "It's almost time for the countdown. Let's go see what your mom has planned."

Getting out of his lap is beyond awkward, and I teeter on my heels for a second before gaining my balance. Reaf, Bryce and I walk into the kitchen, or what's better known as Operation Baby Shower. There are journals and phones littering the table. They have been in super planning mode. I'm not sure if I should be excited or scared.

I clear my throat and they don't budge. I honestly don't think they even heard me. I stand there for about a minute to see if they are going to notice that we're in the same room as them.

Finally, Reaf shouts, "Hey."

They all turn around at the loud boom of his voice. They look a bit peeved that they were interrupted. It's not like this is a life or death party. I'm going to have this baby regardless if there's a party or not.

"It's getting close to midnight. What's the plan?" Reaf asks. I admire that he doesn't back down, not even from a group of party planning women. Most guys would be out of their comfort zone in this situation. He crosses his arms and taps his foot, trying to let them know that they need to speed it up.

Maggie sighs. "Alright, alright, we're coming." The four ladies get out of their chairs almost in sync. You can hear all of them screech across the tiled floor at the same time. I wince at the noise, but we are quickly joined by them at the bar.

At the exact same time Dad walks into the kitchen. "Aren't we supposed to toast soon?"

Mom laughs. "Yes. Why is everyone so damn impatient tonight?"

I pipe in then. "Because some of us are insanely tired." I yawn for emphasis. She can't say I'm being dramatic, when the proof is right there.

"Okay," she says. "Let me get the champagne and sparkling grape juice out."

She begins pouring the champagne in the flutes she's had sitting on the counter all day. When she fills five with champagne, and only three with grape juice, Dad gives her a quizzical look. His brows furrowing in disapproval.

"Why are there so many glasses with bubbly in it?" He questions Mom, glancing at the glasses and the group of us "kids."

"Well," Mom starts. "Cami is over 18, and she's staying the night. Maggie and Caroline are above the legal age to drink. And I don't hear Maggie scoffing at the thought of Reaf drinking a glass." She glances at Maggie for confirmation, and Maggie shrugs.

"But we don't even have permission for Cami to drink. What will her father say?" Dad argues.

Laughing Mom says, "Frankly, I don't give a damn what he says or thinks. Cami has been here almost every day since her and Tonya were little. She's practically our daughter, so I'm making the decision to let her have a small glass of champagne to celebrate. You don't honestly think she's never had a drink before, do you?" She widens her stance and squares her shoulders. That's her signature "you're not going to win this argument stance." Dad will do well if he just backs down now.

"I guess you have a point," he says defeated. Smart man... I knew there was a reason Mom kept him around.

Each of us grab a glass, Caroline grabbing two, and head to the living room. Let's hope that Caroline remembers there's alcohol in one of them. Giving David the wrong flute would probably be frowned upon.

We have two minutes to spare, so we stand around in a circle waiting for the time to tick by. David and I are making faces at each other, and everyone else. Laughter filling the living room is definitely my new favorite moment. New friends, old friends, and family. There's nowhere else I'd rather be tonight. We have about fifteen seconds until the clock strikes midnight.

Dad raises his glass to the ceiling, "To the New Year."

The rest of us raise our glasses and yell, "To the New Year." And we all take a sip of our champagne and grape juice.

The countdown on the television gets closer to zero. Five... Four... Three... Two... One... Everyone is screaming Happy New Year and David is popping the little confetti bottles all over the living room. Small scraps of paper littering the floor.

Reaf pulls me to him and kisses me like his life depends on it. His alcohol tinted lips pressed against mine passionately. I see stars, and they aren't the ones being broadcast on TV. His mouth pulls away from mine, and he wraps me in his arms. He whispers, "I love you" in my ear, and I stiffen.

twenty-six

I WAS NOT EXPECTING THAT...AT all. I'm not sure how to respond so I stand, frozen, with my mouth gaping open. A full minute passes, and I can see fear and confusion pass across Reaf's face.

His cheeks are turning pink. "Are you okay, T?"

I shake myself out of my stupor. "Yeah." I back away slowly. "I need a minute." I turn around and almost break out in a full speed run to get to my room.

I didn't realize I could move that quickly at my size. Apparently I just needed a little motivation in the form of a minor freak out. I slam my door and lock it. I'm still trying to catch my breath as I slump against the door and slide my way down to the floor.

There's a few blissful moments before I hear a knock at my door. I hear Reaf's voice through the door. "Tonya... Is everything okay?"

"Yeah," I reply. "I just need a few minutes."

"Did I do something wrong?" There's hurt in his voice, and I hate that I did that.

"I just... Can you just go? I'll call you later." I know this is the coward's way out, but I need to get ahold of my emotions right now. And I can't do that if I'm in the same vicinity as him.

I can feel him through the piece of wood separating us. Like he's in the same exact position I am. "I'll go. But when you call... Please talk to me. We can get past whatever just happened as long as we communicate."

I nod even though I know he can't see me. I need to get a reign on this. I'm not sure how much time passes when there's another knock on the door. "Reaf, I asked you to go."

"It's not Reaf," says a voice I wasn't expecting to hear.

I stand up, turn the knob, and open the door. I'm shocked even more than I was at the sound of Maggie's voice. Standing in my doorway are Maggie, Caroline, Cami, and Mom. I really hope they aren't here to bombard me with questions.

They file into my room, one after the other. Each one taking a seat on my bed, except Cami. She pulls my chair out from under my desk, and rolls it so that it's facing the bed. Then she pushes my shoulders directing me to sit before going to take her place on my bed.

I want to know why they get the comfortable place on my soft mattress, and I get this desk chair that I absolutely loathe. It does nothing for back pain. And I squirm in my seat just a bit to try to situate myself.

My face is squished up, like I smell something bad. I'm not amused by this little stunt, and I want to make sure they know it.

Mom starts off the inquisition. "Why are you in here? And why did you tell Reaf to go home?"

I shake my head. "Everything was a little much. And I needed to get away."

I know my mom is a human lie detector. She's already shaking her head. "I know you're not telling us the truth. You know you can talk to any one of us right?"

I snort. "I might feel that way, if y'all didn't bum rush me at once. How am I supposed to feel like I can talk when you all come in here like women on a mission."

"That's not far from the truth," Cami laughs.

"Not funny, traitor." I fume.

Cami scoots off the bed, sits on her knees, and grabs my hands. She pulls my chair toward her. "Ignore everyone else. Talk to me. What happened? Everything was fine one minute, and the next you were missing in action."

I sigh. "Right after Reaf wished me a happy new year, he said he loved me, and I freaked out. It just seems like it's so fast. We've barely been seeing each other for a month, and he chooses tonight to tell me this? And with his family present? I felt sort of trapped. I didn't know how to respond, so I ran."

I can feel the salty tears run down my cheeks. I didn't expect to feel this much when only moments ago I was fuming at them interrupting my brooding. I'm not sure what all they can say to make things any better. But they are all older, well, except for Cami, and maybe they have some words of wisdom.

Cami says, "Oh sweetheart. I think I would have reacted the same exact way. But maybe these ladies have a bit more advice for you."

I expect Mom to speak up first, but it's Maggie. "Sweetie, I know I haven't known you very long, but you are a lovely young woman. And when Reaf loves, he loves fiercely. I know he cares about you, and he wouldn't have expected you to say anything back out of obligation. But you should talk to him. Explain why you got upset, and figure out what to do from there."

I'm sobbing so hard I can't speak. After such a short time, I adore his mom. And right now, I feel like I'm letting her down. "Di-di-did he leave?"

Caroline shakes her head. "No, he's in the kitchen with your dad and Bryce. I'm sure he's trying to figure out how to make this better."

When I don't say anything, Mom looks around at all three of them and asks, "Can y'all leave me alone with Tonya for a moment?"

They don't say anything as they get up and start for my door. Each woman giving me a reassuring pat or squeeze on my shoulder before they walk out of my room.

Mom pats the space next to her on my bed. I do as she asks and sink into the warmth left by Caroline. I lean my head on my Mom's shoulder and wait to see what she's going to say.

She wraps her arm around me and pulls me closer to her. "It's okay to be scared of emotions, especially right now when yours are all over the place, mija. But how you handled things wasn't very nice. Relationships are hard. They take work. It's not all sunshine and rainbows all the time."

I nod. "I know that. I just didn't know what else to do. I like Reaf a lot. Well, more than just like him. I can see myself falling for him, but the "L" word is terrifying. I thought I loved Jake, and that he loved me, but we both ended up hurt.

I don't want that to happen to either of us. I just can't tell if I would feel the same way about him if I wasn't pregnant."

Mom gives me a tight squeeze. "Then talk to him. Explain how you're feeling. I'm going to go grab him, and send him in here. You need to talk."

I grin. "Are you actually allowing a boy in my room?"

She just laughs. "It's not like I have to worry about anything happening." She glances at my stomach, and then looks at me and winks.

I throw a pillow at her retreating back. While I wait for the awkward conversation that's about to happen, I grab my phone off the nightstand. With all the fun we were having earlier, I didn't even check my phone. I didn't feel a need to have it within reach at all tonight. Looking at the notifications, I notice that Jake text me. I'm a little shocked, and don't know what is waiting for me in my messages box.

Just as I'm about to open up the message, Reaf knocks on the frame of my door. He looks sheepish, and a little lost. I feel horrible for making him doubt himself.

I look up at him, my cheeks blushing. "You can come in."

He walks toward where I'm sitting but doesn't sit down. I guess he's kind of scared to after my little run away stunt earlier. I pat the space next to me, and Reaf takes a seat. But he doesn't sit too close. I think he's preparing for the worst.

"I'm sorry, Tonya. I shouldn't have surprised you with those three words. I imagined that going so differently." He's rambling, and speaking so fast I can barely understand him.

I grab his hand. "No, don't apologize. I shouldn't have freaked out. I didn't know what to say after you told me, and

I wish I could use a time turner to go back and handle it differently."

He laughs, "Always a *Harry Potter* reference where you can fit one in."

"I can't help it," I giggle. "When you've read it as much as I have, it becomes difficult to not make a reference at least once a day."

I'm still gripping his hand like my life depends on it. "I just need a little bit of time. I care about you... a lot. I'm not sure if it's the beginnings of love, but hearing you say those words, kind of scared the shit out of me. Can we rewind and try to take things a little slower?"

"Absolutely," he says while nodding. "I'll give you as much time as you need. Just talk to me. I know your last relationship was a bit rocky, but talk to me. I won't get mad. Your feelings are just as valid as mine. But don't think I won't keep trying to win your heart over. You're my future, Tonya. I don't know what I would do without you in my life. You're an inspiration, and I hope one day you'll feel the same way about me that I feel about you."

"Thanks for that," I sigh. "I was worried you would hate me. And I don't think I could live with that."

"Never," he says, and he's gripping my hands now instead of the other way around. "I'm going to go ahead and go. It's getting late, and I don't want to be on the road with all the other crazies out celebrating tonight."

He leans over and gives me a quick peck on the lips. I want to deepen the kiss, but I know that won't be fair to him. I just told him I need time, and I can't mess that up by giving in to my desires. Instead, I hug him like he's the anchor I need to stay stable on this rocky terrain my life will become.

After he leaves, I start to pull down the comforter so I can get ready to fall asleep. When I remember the text from Jake. I set my phone on the nightstand without opening it. Whatever it is can be dealt with tomorrow. Right now I need to sleep. And try to figure out how much I feel for Reaf.

twenty-seven

IT'S BEEN ALMOST two weeks since I received that text from Jake, and I'm still not sure how to process it. All it said was "I'm not going to give you any more problems." That was it, nothing else. I'm happy that he's going to stop trying to get me back. But what does that mean about everything else?

I text him back, but he never replied. I guess I deserve the silent treatment after I did the same to him. But it sucks. Is he going to be here for Little Bean? I'm hoping he will, but I worry that he won't want to be in her life. Even when he was harassing me to get back with him, he never once mentioned what was going to be good for our daughter. Hell, he doesn't even know that he's having a daughter yet.

On top of that, I'm still confused about Reaf. He's kept to his word and backed off a bit. That doesn't mean we don't still talk every day, but not quite as much. And things haven't been as intimate, which means no "L" word. I miss how things were, but I'm happy he actually listened to my needs. Gah, why do relationships have to be so fucking confusing.

The only bright spot is my baby shower this weekend. Cami and Mom have been working hard on making sure I have the perfect party. As far as I know, Reaf's mom and sister are still coming. I'm not sure if he is, yet. Mom hasn't said. She's been kind of quiet on the whole Reaf topic so that she doesn't set me into another emotional tailspin.

The shower will be a little bittersweet for me. I'll get to celebrate my still unnamed Little Bean, but Cami leaves for school again. She seems to be doing better after our pep talk on Christmas, but I'm not sure if it's just for me, or if she's trying to be strong for herself. I guess time will tell. I just know that I'm going to miss her after seeing her almost every day for a month.

I'm sitting in the living room surrounded by pink and black crepe paper. I even have one of those "Mommy To-Be" sashes on. I would never do this for anyone except for my mother and Cami. They wanted me to wear a Super Mom cape with pacifiers and bottles glued to it, but I had to draw the line somewhere. The sash is more than enough. I even dressed up a bit. I'm wearing a shift dress with floral prints and sandals even though it's ridiculously cold outside. But that's the beauty of being pregnant, I don't have to go outside if I don't want to.

The room is buzzing with energy and that's only coming off the two hosts because nobody else has gotten here yet. Mom keeps telling me there is a mystery guest, and I'm nervous to see who it could be. There's very few people I would be excited to see.

I wander into the kitchen under the guise of seeing if they need any help. But really, I just want to sneak some of the snacks. Honestly, how can you have an amazing spread of food that includes vegetables, cupcakes, candy, and chocolate, and just pass by it without sampling it.

I'm about to steal a second carrot when it's slapped out of my hand. I turn to my mom. "You know I have to eat that right? I touched it. There are germs on it. My germs, which means I should eat it."

She rolls her eyes. "Fine, eat the damn carrot, then get out of the kitchen."

"Geez Mom. What's your problem? It's not like this whole routine isn't normal for me," I laugh trying to get her to calm down.

She slumps against the counter. "I know, sweetie. I'm sorry. It's just that your super special guest was supposed to be here already, and she's not." Shrugging she says, "Now let's get you back to the living room. I hear your favorite chair calling your name. People should start arriving any minute."

I don't really want to leave Mom when she's looking stressed, but I know if I just listen that will help with her anxiety level. I'm just lowering myself into my chair when the doorbell rings. Cami runs to it so that I'm not tempted to get back up. It's Caroline and Maggie. They give me a quick peck on the cheek, set their gifts on the table, and go see what my mom needs help with.

Before long the house is full of women. Some I haven't seen since graduation, people I would hang out with and considered casual friends. They are all home on break. A few of my aunts and cousins are here. And I'm excited to see them. I see them pretty regularly, but with school, work and pregnancy in general I haven't made it a priority like I used to.

We're all getting settled to play the first game of the party. Well, more like game that lasts the entire party. You have to put a safety pin on, and anytime you hear someone say baby, you take their pin. Whoever has the most pins at the end of the party wins. Mom is explaining this to everyone, and I hear a knock at the door. Cami rushes to the door to see who's here.

She calls out excitedly, leaving the door wide open. "She's here!"

Mom stops her explanation of the game mid-sentence and rushes to the door. When she comes back around the corner she's in front of someone trying to block my view of who is behind her.

Finally, I catch a glimpse of the person she's hiding, and I burst out in tears of pure happiness. My great-grandmother made the trip to celebrate this little person I'll be giving birth to soon. I could not be happier. I wasn't expecting her to show up. She's not exactly young and spry anymore. But she will always be my favorite person in the world. I have so many great memories of her throughout my childhood. Making tortillas together, her teaching me how to sew and crochet. I don't think I'd be the person I am today without her hand in my life.

"Lala, you made it," I manage to squeak out.

"Of course, mija," She says. The joy in seeing me evident

in her voice. "I wouldn't miss the party for your first baby, even if she wasn't exactly planned."

I look into her eyes, and see they are just as watery as mine. I would do anything for her, and I think I may have a name in mind to honor her.

I lead her to my favorite chair, and motion for her to sit. She tries to object, but I won't hear it. After she's situated I start to lower myself to the floor beside her, but there's a chair pushed next to her and I couldn't be more grateful.

The games are a pain. I begged Mom not to play any, but as usual, my vote didn't count. At least she didn't do the "Poo in the Diaper" game. That just seems gross. Blegh. A few of my friends won prizes, and I'm starting to get antsy. I'm not used to being around this many people anymore. I think I've slowly started becoming an introvert throughout this pregnancy.

Finally, we are at the part of the shower when I get to open presents. I know they aren't for me but it's still ridiculously fun to tear apart wrapping paper. I get a slew of things that I didn't even think I would need. There are a ton of receiving blankets, a Moby wrap, and a couple of different diaper bags. And the clothes... I have no idea how this child is going to wear all of them.

Lala hands me her gift, and I do my best to be gentle with it. It feels soft and cushiony. When I open it, I see a beautiful crocheted blanket. It's a rosy pink and cream color alternating between rows. Mom must have told her I was having a girl Christmas night. There's no other way she would have had time to make this.

I hug the blanket to my chest, and lean over to give her a

hug. "Thank you, Lala. This means a lot to me and Little Bean."

"De nada, Mija," she whispers, and squeezes me to her. I squeeze her back and pour all my love into that one small gesture.

Everyone is getting ready to leave, and I thank everyone for coming and for the gifts I've received. Lala is staying the night because my aunt that brought her doesn't want to drive back in the same day. It's a four-hour drive and that's taxing on anybody.

While Mom is getting the guest room situated, Caroline and Maggie come tell me goodbye. But before they leave Caroline places a small box in my hands.

"It's from Reaf," she says. "He didn't want to make things awkward by coming by, but he asked me to give you this."

"Thank you." I say, tearing up again. Ugh, stupid pregnancy hormones have me bawling like a baby at the most inopportune times.

I sit in the chair that my great-grandmother just vacated and slowly pull the ribbon off the box. I open the lid, and see two concert tickets sitting on top of a folded piece of paper. They are tickets to a music festival I mentioned wanting to attend once. Now, I can't hold back the tears. He pays attention to all the small things, and my heart swells.

Under the tickets is a note written in his neat handwriting.

Dear T,

I remember you mentioning wanting to go to this concert. I know it's a month after you have Little Bean, but I hope you can make it. There are two tickets so that you can take whoever you'd like. Though, I'm secretly hoping it will be me.

I'm sure you received a ton of things for your little girl at the shower, but this is for you. Just because you're becoming a mom doesn't mean you need to forget who you are. You can be both people. Don't let anyone tell you differently. I've already made sure you'll have a sitter for Little Bean that day. Mom and Caroline are going to hang out with your mom and watch her.

I hope you had a great baby shower, and if you need any help putting things together or sorting through it all, let me know. I'm here for you in any way that you'll let me. Just know that I care about you, and only want the best for you and your daughter.

With love,

Reaf

I've gone from crying to all out sobbing. This guy makes my heart burst, and I've been trying to keep him at arm's length. I can't deny that I have stronger feelings for him than just like. I might even possibly love him. But how can I be sure?

I pad into the kitchen to see if my great-grandmother is around. If there's one thing I've learned, it's that she has a lot of wisdom. She has always known what to say to put my fears at ease. It appears I'm in luck. She's sitting at the kitchen table with a cup of coffee between her hands.

I pull out the chair next to her, and wait. I'm trying to gather my thoughts, and I'm not exactly sure where to start.

Lala puts her hand on my arm. "What's wrong, mi Corazon? You look sad."

I sigh, and place my free hand over hers on my arm. "Nothing and everything. I'm just really confused and feel lost."

"This sounds like a boy problem," she laughs.

"You have no idea," I grumble. "How do you know when you're in love with someone. Not the fluffy puppy love stuff, but *real* love?"

"Mija, it's not something you can explain," she pauses for a couple of seconds. "It's something you feel... in here." She raises her hand and puts it against my chest where my heart is.

"But I thought I felt that way before. And it got me hurt. This time it feels like more, and that terrifies me." I argue.

"Love is scary... And it's not easy. You have to work for it." She raises my chin so she can look into my eyes. "Does this boy make you feel different? Does being away from him make you long for him?"

I nod. Blinking back the tears trying to form. "Yes. Since he came into my life, it feels like everything is upside down. I thought everything was going fine when I was on my own, but he makes me want more. For myself, and for Little Bean."

The smile on Lala's face is exuberant. "Then you love him, Mija. Don't let fear and confusion push him away. Take his love and run with it. Be happy."

I give her a giant bear hug. I don't know what I would do without her wisdom. I know if I had gotten this same advice from Mom, I probably would have mocked her. Maybe it's because my great-grandmother has so much life experience, but her words calm me, and I know what I need to do now.

When I get to my room, Cami is sitting on the bed. She has the concert tickets in her hand and glances up at me as soon as I walk in. I can tell from the guilty expression on her face that she read the letter, too.

"As much as I would *love* to go to this concert with you, please tell me you're taking Reaf. That letter was the sweetest thing I've ever read." She's sniffling, and that's something I've never seen her do. She's always been my rock when I have emotional breakdowns, but his words must have affected her as well.

I scoff. "Of course, I'm going to take Reaf. How can I not after that letter and just how amazing he's been? It would be pretty shitty if I didn't take him."

Just then my phone rings and I dig it out of my pocket. With all of my emotions jumbled, I don't bother looking at the screen to see who it is.

"Hello," I answer.

"Can we talk?" A voice says through the receiver. Except it's not the one I'm expecting... It's Jake.

twenty-eight

I STAND STOCK STILL. That's not the voice I was longing to hear, but I guess I should be happy Jake is finally returning my call. I just hope he's not going back on his word to leave me alone about us being together.

"Um, yeah...s-s-sure," I stutter. "What's up?"

I'm trying to regain my composure, but honestly this call after that weird text has thrown me for a loop. I don't know whether to be relieved or pissed.

"Well, I'm not trying to get back with you, so you can go ahead and get that thought out of your head. I can see you're happy with Reaf, and it would be selfish of me to try to take that away from you." He says, resigned.

Color me shocked. That's not what I was expecting, either.

"It's about the baby..." He starts, but doesn't finish the rest of his thought.

"What about her?" I ask.

"Her? The baby's a girl? That's... That's good to hear. I wasn't sure if you found out yet. Anyway, I'm getting off track. I know you want me to be in her life, but I don't know if I'm ready for that. I'm still trying to wrap my head around the fact that I'm going to be a father. I know I've had a while to do that, but it didn't seem *real* until I saw you. Honestly, I'm fucking scared as hell."

I roll my eyes. I get where he's coming from, but this probably isn't a conversation to have over the phone.

"Well," I begin. "I'm scared too, but I don't have the option of running away. This little girl will depend on me, on us, to make a great life for her. She's going to need you just as much as she needs me. Are you sure you want to give up on being a dad?"

I hear a sniffle on the other end of the line. Is he crying? Maybe I'm being a little too hard on him. I've dealt with this reality for the past six months. He hasn't had to face this pregnancy daily.

He sniffs again. "No, I'm not saying I want to give it up completely. I just need time. To get my head on straight, and to be the person she can look up to."

"That's admirable Jake. But how long is that going to take? Months? Years? What am I supposed to tell our daughter when she asks about her father?" I ask.

"You have Reaf, right? He can help."

I laugh, bitterly. "No, that's not fair to Little Bean or Reaf. I can't ask that of him. I'm sure he would take care of her as if she were his own, but she's not his responsibility."

Cami walks over to put her arms around me. She can tell by the sound of my voice that I'm panicking. I couldn't be more grateful to her than I am right now. She always has my back, even when she doesn't know what is going on.

Jake replies, "I know, I know. Damn it. I don't really

want him to take my place, but I don't know what to do. Please, just give me some time. Or at least think about it. You don't even have to put my last name on her birth certificate until I can prove myself a fit father. And when I do... We can go through the process of giving her my last name."

"I'll think about it," I sigh, defeated. "I have to go." I hang up the phone before he has a chance to reply.

Crumpling to the floor I let my tears flow. How is it that my happiness at my revelation of loving Reaf can come down so quickly just by speaking to Little Bean's father? Cami continues to hold me while texting someone from my phone. I'm too worn out to care who she's talking to.

Just when I've got my emotions under control and can finally breathe again, Reaf rushes into my room and crashes to the floor beside me. So that's who she messaged... Cami slowly backs away to sit on my bed when Reaf throws his arms around me. I can't stop the emotions from bubbling back up. And I'm crying again. When will these outbursts stop? I feel like I've got a split personality lately. Reaf is muttering soothing words into my ear while he brushes my hair back from my face.

I pull back. "Why are you here?" I hiccup.

He shrugs, "Cami said you needed me, so I came right over."

I hug him tighter. "You didn't have to do that." I sigh. "I don't deserve you."

I can feel him shaking his head above mine. "You don't get to decide if you deserve me or not. I told you how I feel about you, and that's all there is to it."

"Now, tell me what has you spiraling out of control," he says as he sits back on his heels.

I recount the entire conversation to Cami and Reaf. I see their shock, and understanding. But understanding for whom? Me, or Jake? By the time I'm winding down the conversation I feel deflated. I don't think I could handle one more thing on my plate than what I have right now.

Reaf opens his mouth cautiously, like he's scared of how I'm going to react to his words. "Maybe you should consider what Jake said." I'm about to go off on a wild tangent, but Reaf puts his forefinger to my mouth to shush me. "Hear me out. This is huge for him. He hasn't been here going through the daily grind with you. He doesn't understand the sacrifice that taking care of a child entails."

"But why should I have to do it all alone?" I argue.

Cami pipes in. "Who says you're going to do it alone? Do you not remember you have two parents that are more than willing to help you along the way? Or that I will help you as much as I can? I'm your best friend. If there's anyone you should count on, it's me."

"I know," I mumble. "But what about when you're away at school. Did you forget that you leave tomorrow?"

"I sure as hell didn't forget." She says, indignant. "But you also have Reaf to be your shoulder to lean on while I'm away. And if he fails at that job, I know where the gardening shears are." She winks at Reaf, and he winces. She's all bark with no bite, but I'm not sure that he knows that.

When did my friend and sort-of boyfriend decide to gang up on me? I'm not sure how I feel about that, but I'm happy they are in my corner. "I guess I will consider it. I just don't want to lie to Little Bean about her father."

"Then don't," Reaf replies. "Tell her who her father is, show her pictures of him. I have a feeling he'll come around and be the dad he needs to be. But you don't have to lie to her until he figures it out."

"What do I do if she asks why her Daddy didn't want her?" I ask.

"You tell her that he does. He just needs a little time to be the perfect Dad for her." Cami says with conviction.

I grab my phone off the floor where Cami left it and text Jake. I need to do this before I overthink the entire situation.

Me: *You have your time. Don't let our daughter down.*
Jake: *Thank you...*

I don't reply to his last text. I set my phone aside and get off the floor, carefully. It gets harder the further along in the pregnancy I am.

I reach for Reaf's hand to indicate that I want him to get up. "I have someone I'd like you to meet."

Even though her approval isn't completely necessary, I want my great-grandmother to meet the man who has stolen my heart.

* * *

I can't believe it's already time to say goodbye to Lala and Cami. I'm going to miss them both so much. Lala is heading back home, but I promised her I would come see her after the baby is born. She has to take her to get her ears pierced, after all. It's a tradition she started with her granddaughters and one I want her to continue with my daughter.

Cami is going back to life in the dorms, and hopefully finding a way to stand up to her father while continuing to attend school. I just hope she doesn't let my words of encouragement fall to the back burner.

Lala *loved* Reaf. Not that I didn't think she would. I'm just happy that I have her support if things progress further with him. Any person who wins my great-grandmother's heart is a person to keep around. She doesn't give it freely to others easily.

It's just me and my parents now. It's time to get all the baby gear put away, and get ready for my semester of online courses. I need to let my professors know that I'll be giving birth soon, and I hope they are understanding. Until it happens, I'll do my best to get ahead in all of my classes so that I don't fall behind when it's time for Little Bean to make her arrival.

twenty-nine

SO FAR THIS semester has been easier to manage than the last one. I think the online courses are helping with that. It has been a relief not having to rush to class after work. It definitely makes my days less stressful.

I communicated with all of my professors that I would be having a baby in the next few weeks, and all of them have been very supportive. The joy of online classes... You pretty much get to work at your own pace. Though, they've said they will allow me extensions to accommodate whatever my schedule may be post birth. I could not be more grateful.

It's been three weeks since my baby shower, and everything is perfect so far. I've been spending a lot more time with Reaf. He'll either come to my house when we're off work, or I'll go to his. Most of those nights are spent studying, sadly. And when we're at Reaf's, David doesn't give us much time to be alone. He's taken a liking to me, and I'm okay with that. He's adorable, and I have a feeling him and Little Bean will be the best of friends.

Tonight we are at my house watching *Valentine's Day*.

It's one of my favorite movies, even when I'm not single. There's something to be learned from this movie, love comes in many shapes and forms. Sometimes we just need other people to show us a little bit of kindness.

I'm not sure what Reaf has planned for Valentine's Day, but knowing him it will be something romantic and epic. I've learned to expect the unexpected when it comes to his actions.

He slides his arm around me, and I snuggle further into his warmth. I can feel my happiness increase just by being in his presence. He's gliding his fingers over my arm and I feel tingles all the way to my toes. In the two years I spent with Jake, I *never* felt this way, and I'm beyond happy that I'm finally feeling it with a guy that gets me. And accepts me completely.

The movie is about halfway over when I feel a sharp pain in my pelvis area. I blow it off because I've been feeling this off and on for the past couple of weeks. Mom says they are Braxton Hicks since none of them are consistent. They just come and go.

When the movie is over I get another pang of pain. I wince at the feel of it. Maybe I should be a little worried now. Mom and Dad are out at dinner and going to a movie. I'm not sure what to do. Reaf must notice my sudden discomfort because he moves as fast and easily as he can to bend down in front of me.

Worry is written all over his face. "What's wrong?"

"I think I'm having contractions. I felt the first one about 30 minutes ago, and I just had another one." I say, trying to catch my breath.

"I'm going to grab a notebook from your room and my

phone. I think we should start timing them. When are your parents supposed to be home?" He asks.

"I'm not sure. They wanted to get in one more date night before their lives become consumed by their grandchild."

I stand up and start walking around to try to alleviate the pressure. My water hasn't broken, at least I don't think it has, so that must be a good sign. Reaf is back with the notebook and phone. I can see writing at the top of the page. Why didn't I research how labor would feel? All I've seen from movies and TV shows is a gush of water right before the woman starts screaming bloody murder. I don't want that to be me.

I'm still pacing when I double over in pain. I try to do the breathing techniques I learned in the one Lamaze class I went to. I thought they were useless classes, now I wish I had stuck with them.

Reaf is behind me in a second. "Deep breath in... Now let it out. That one came faster than the last one. Maybe I should call your parents."

"No, don't do that," I say while trying to maintain my breathing. "What if this is a false alarm? I don't want them to end their date night and come home just to realize that I'm not having a baby yet."

"Sweetheart," he says while rubbing my arms to keep me calm. "I don't think this is a false alarm. Do you want me to call Caroline instead?"

"Yes, call her," I pant.

Reaf leaves the room to call his sister, and I sit on the floor hoping it will help some. It doesn't, I feel like it makes the uncomfortable pain worse. So I start pacing again.

Another contraction hits. It's only been fifteen minutes since the last one. Holy shit. How am I going to push a baby out?

My breathing is quickening, and I'm on the edge of a panic attack. This can't be good if I'm going into labor. Where's Reaf? He was just going to call his sister. What's taking him so long? I don't think I can deal with this alone.

Finally, he rushes back into the living room. "My sister said we should go ahead and go to the hospital. Don't get mad," he prefaces his next words. "But I called your parents. They are an hour away, but will meet us in labor and delivery."

"Damn it, Reaf. I told you not to call them." I whine. But honestly, I'm relieved he had the foresight to call them. Even when I'm thinking irrationally he's there to even it out.

Reaf disappears into my room. I hear doors and drawers being opened and closed. I slowly make my way toward my room. It's still painted a light shade of pink from my childhood. I think after the Bean gets here, it'll be time for an update. And wow, my mind just kind of took off there for a minute.

I glance at Reaf. He looks like Taz the cartoon character whirling about my room. "What are you doing?" I ask barely masking the giggle that's working its way out of my mouth.

"I am trying to get you a bag ready to go to the hospital. What does it look like?" He says, impatient.

"You don't have to do that."

He sounds exasperated, "Yes, I do. You aren't doing anything and we need to go."

"No, really, you don't," I laugh. "My bag is right inside the closet door, and Little Bean's is in her crib."

I can feel the tension leave him, even from across the room. "Why didn't you tell me that before?"

I shrug. "You didn't ask."

Reaf breezes by me, grabs the bag out of my closet and then leaves the room. I hear him in Bean's room and then the door shuts soon after.

He peeks back into my room. "Are you coming?"

"Yep," I say. Just as I leave the room, another contraction hits. I grab on to the door jamb and breathe through it. Why didn't anyone tell me these contractions would be painful?

Reaf comes back to help me get to the car as quickly as possible. "Why aren't we taking mine?" I ask.

"Because," he says, "I don't like driving that death trap. It only drives well for you, and I'm not chancing it tonight."

Reaf drives like the hounds of Hell are after him. I think we make it to the hospital in ten minutes flat. But I can't be sure. The contractions seem like they are coming faster and more painful. I have a death grip on the "oh shit" handle at the top of the car. I wouldn't be surprised if there are nail marks on the console after I get out.

He pulls the car into the emergency loop, parks, and gets out to help me out of the car. As I get out, the next contraction almost brings me to my knees. Just as Reaf is trying to help me up, my mom runs out of the emergency room.

"I never should have tried to have a date night so close to your due date. You are early, though." Relief evident in her voice.

"How did you beat us here?" I ask.

Reaf chimes in, "Because someone wouldn't get in gear and get out of the house." He tilts his head in my direction, signaling my parents that it's my fault. Okay, so maybe I take some of the blame.

Mom and Dad lead me in to the emergency room, Reaf trailing behind us. The waiting area is bright and smells like disinfectant. Ugh, can't they make this place a little more uplifting? Maybe when people come in they wouldn't be so depressed. This place needs some color.

Mom is at the information desk getting me checked in, and Reaf my ever present knight, is by my side helping me breathe through the contractions that are getting more intense with each passing minute.

Mom comes back to us and lets us know they are getting the room ready. "They want to know who you want in the room, sweetie." She says while gauging how I'm going to take that statement.

"Just you, Mom. Reaf and I aren't at that level yet," I glance at him to make sure he's not taking offense. He just smiles and nods. I continue, "And it would be a little awkward with Dad in there."

"Okay, I'll go let the nurses know," Mom says as she turns around.

I pull Reaf to the side. "Can you call Cami and Jake to let them know I'm in labor? Their names are in my phone under 'Bestie' and 'Jackass'."

He laughs. "Absolutely. I'll be in there with you as soon as you have Little Bean."

He gives me a quick kiss on the cheek and I'm on my way to have this child. Please don't let it hurt.

* * *

Fucking hell. I was not expecting that level of pain. It was intense and amazing at the same time. It's such a weird combination. But I am quite possibly the happiest lady in the world right now. My daughter is in my arms, sleeping like the angel she is. I just hope she likes to sleep just like her mama.

Mom has already tried to hog her and that's not going to happen. I went through nine months of being uncomfortable and that immense pain. I'm going to hang on to the little person that has turned my world upside down.

Reaf is by my side. Making funny faces at her sweet little face even though she's sleeping and can't see that far. I'm humming *Twinkle, Twinkle Little Star* and she smiles contentedly.

I look over to Reaf. "Can you take a picture of her for me? I'm at an awkward angle."

He smiles at me. "Absolutely." He takes the picture then hands me the phone.

I send a text to Cami and Jake.

Please welcome Miss Layla Marie Burgess to the world.

Cami couldn't make it because she has a final in the morning. But Jake wants to come see her when he's home for Spring Break.

I get responses back from both of them saying the same exact thing.

She's beautiful.

I feel like I can take on the world surrounded by most of the people I love. Yes, even Reaf. I haven't told him yet, but I think he knows.

Little Layla and I are ready to start our new future.

epilogue

LAYLA IS JUST over a month old, and I'm nervous about leaving her already. I'll be back home tonight, but it feels weird being somewhere she isn't. Mom assured me that she'll be fine while Reaf and I are gone. I made her promise she would call me if my Little Bean started being too much for them to handle. She chastised me for not trusting her parenting skills.

It's the day of the music festival, and though I was weary about leaving Layla, I'm excited to see some of my favorite bands with the guy I adore and love. Reaf and I fight to find a parking spot.

It's still a little chilly this morning for early Spring, so I have a light sweater over my tank top, and shorts so that I'm comfortable. Reaf is wearing his signature jeans and white shirt. His hat turned backward. There are people everywhere. I didn't expect there to be so many bodies in one space. We make our way to a blank area in the field and set our blanket out.

I lean back and soak in the sun while listening to great

live music. Walk the Moon is on the stage and starts playing their song *Shut Up and Dance*. This may be my favorite song of all time.

I can feel Reaf staring at me even though my eyes are closed. Before the song gets to the chorus, he's tugging my arm trying to get me to stand up.

"Dance with me," he says, placing his arms around my waist. It feels odd now they finally fit all the way around me with room to spare.

"Anytime, and anywhere," I tell him. Grinning like a fool.

Grouplove begins playing as soon as Walk the Moon finishes, and they open with *Welcome to Your Life*. I can't help thinking it's the perfect song to let Reaf know how I feel.

I have my arms around his neck, and pull him closer to me so that my lips reach his ear. "I love you," I whisper.

I'm not even surprised when he whispers back, "I know."

The road ahead may be bumpy, and though I didn't care for Reaf when I first met him. He somehow snuck his way into my heart and made me love him. I'm ready to see where this new life takes us.

Did you enjoy Tonya & Reaf's story? Sign up for my newsletter for the original prologue and scenes from Reaf and Jake's point of view!

You can also grab a copy of Tonya and Reaf's wedding story, From This Moment!

* * *

Prologue

I hear the party raging around me. Red Dirt Rock blaring from the speakers in the living room. The haze of smoke hanging in the air. I can't remember exactly where I am, except that I'm at some frat party. All I know is I'm in the bathroom trying to put myself back together.

I know better than to mix alcohol with my anxiety meds, but right now I don't care. I need to throw this whole "Little Miss Perfect" persona out the window. That's not who I am, not really. It's what I let everyone else see. The only exception would be Tonya, and she's not here to pick me back up again. Inside, I'm a mess. I'm filled with anxiety, insecurities, and an unbreakable need to self-destruct. I'm a ticking time bomb... just waiting to explode.

I remember when I was a child and had nothing expected of me. As long as I did well in school and stayed out of trouble, I could do whatever I wanted. I'm not sure when all that changed, but I wish I could go back to those carefree days more than anything.

I scan the bathroom trying to find something to dry my hands. There's mold in the creases of the bathtub, dried toothpaste in the sink and splattered across the mirror. You can definitely tell these are guys that don't care about appearances. I can only imagine what my perfect and pristine mother would say about the state of this space. Not to mention how the rest of the house looks, with cups and empty bottles scattered across it.

I feel another bout of sickness hit me and rush to lean my head over the toilet. I heave up everything that's left in my stomach. This is the *last* time I'll do this. I say that, but we all know this time next week, I'll be back in the same position.

Someone's banging on the door causing me to look up. I glance at the door, but another round of sickness hits me. They're just going to have to wait. I'm not moving from this spot, and they can't get through the door. That's when I hear his voice, and assume he's the one trying to get in.

"Cami," Travis yells through the piece of wood separating us. "I know you're in there. Open the damn door."

I blink my eyes, trying to process what he just said. For some unknown reason, Travis thinks he has to look out for me. He found me in pretty much the same state a week ago.

Since then, he's shown up at almost every party I've attended. I don't know why he won't leave me alone. We aren't even friends. We have a few classes together. That doesn't make him my fucking keeper. Besides, he doesn't have much room to treat me like I'm a kid. Any time I've seen him, he's hanging out with the academic kids that dare to come to these parties.

I try to stand up...slowly. The bathroom isn't that big and it shouldn't take this much effort. Grabbing the sink for support, I turn to unlock the door. A wave of dizziness comes over me, and I stumble. I reach for anything that will help catch my fall, but my fingers slip off every object I attempt to grasp.

As the lights begin to fade around me, I hear Travis calling my name. "Cami... Cami." It sounds like he's out of breath. "Damn it, why do you keep doing this?"

And everything goes black.

deleted scenes

ONE

prologue from jake's point of view

FREEDOM! That's the only word on repeat inside my head. Hanging out with my fellow classmates around a huge ass fire is the perfect way to end senior year. Tonight, I'm going to let loose, and celebrate the reprieve I'll have from my parents in a few short months. Being their son isn't easy and I can't wait to be away from them.

The only thing that would make it better is Tonya going to the same school as me. She has her own plans, and dreams, but I can't help the frustration over her not even considering it. She'd rather go to the same school as Cami, and I'm not going to lie...that hurts.

Hell, even now, at our last big celebration after walking across the stage, she's not by my side. These parties aren't her thing, but she could suck it up just once to celebrate the end of this chapter of our lives.

Dylan is going on and on about his latest out of town conquest. He never dates anyone from our school. It's weird, and I honestly doubt any of these girls actually exist. I'm not about to say that, though. Especially when we've been drinking and have a good buzz going for us.

Tonya's voice floats over the low rumble of conversations. "I'm ready to go." Surely, she's not talking to me. We haven't even been here that long. She taps me on the shoulder. "I said I'm ready to go, Jake."

Turning around, I stumble a bit. I guess I've put away a few more beers than I realized. "Well, I'm not. Go hang out with Cami, or something." How dare she do this tonight. Every single time we go to a party, she wants to leave instead of hanging out with everyone. Not. Tonight.

Her shoulders are set, and her back is straight. She's not going to let this go. "Cami is hooking up with some guy. It's hot, and I'm tired of standing around."

"Too damn bad, Tonya. I'm not leaving so chill the fuck out," I yell. If this wasn't a constant, or our graduation party, it'd be different. It's the norm, and I'm not backing down this time.

Instead of storming off like she usually does, she gets in my face. "Who the hell do you think you are? We've been dating a long time, but that does not mean you can talk to me like I'm worthless." She takes a deep breath. "I'm leaving, and I don't care if I have to walk all the way home," she screams. "I'm tired of this shit, and can't take it anymore."

She walks toward the barely visible driveway in the middle of the field. That's the reaction I was expecting a few moments ago. I didn't expect her to essentially end things with me in front of the entire damn party.

"That's okay, bitch, keep walking. Now I don't have to deal with your moody ass anymore," I laugh.

She stops dead in her tracks. One second. Two. She turns long enough to flip me off, and starts walking again.

Regret fills me with her parting gesture. Did I seriously just say that to her and laugh? I wanted to do something to piss her off, but I didn't think before I said it.

"Dude," Randall says. "You're better off without her dragging you down."

"Yeah," I chuckle. It's not funny. Not even a little bit. I just ruined everything with the only bright spot in my life. The one person who could calm me down after getting into arguments with my parents. I fucked up and I know there's no way of fixing it.

original prologue for welcome to your life

THERE'S nothing like sitting around a bonfire in the beginning of summer. It's already hot as Hades, and this whole shindig is ridiculous. I know it's supposed to be our last big party since we graduated a few hours ago, but I'm pretty much over it. It's the same people and the same place. Doesn't anyone get tired of seeing each other all the damn time?

I'm in shorts and a tank top, standing as far away from the monstrosity of flames as I can, and I'm still sweating. I'm surprised the police haven't been called out here by concerned neighbors. The flames are definitely high enough to be seen from town. But I guess being in the middle of a field on private property keeps that from happening. Jake and his buddies didn't plan this well at all. We should be at a pool somewhere, or hell, even the lake. Everyone thought it was a great idea since the star athlete suggested it. I told him otherwise, and he acted as if I never even opened my mouth.

Jake is standing with a few of his friends and I'm

heading toward him. I don't feel like being here anymore. I'd much rather be at home, curled up in bed and reading a book.

"I'm ready to go," I tell Jake when I reach him. He completely ignores me, like he always does when we're at these parties. Don't get me wrong he's a nice guy, but when he starts drinking, he goes into asshole mode.

I tap him on the arm, "I said I'm ready to go, Jake."

He whirls around on me. And I can already tell by that glazed look in his eyes that he's going to be a jerk.

"Well, I'm not. Go hang out with Cami, or something." He glares at me, daring me to argue with him.

"Cami is hooking up with some guy. It's hot, and I'm tired of standing around." I know I should keep my mouth closed but I don't like being told what to do.

"Too damn bad, Tonya. I'm not leaving, so chill the fuck out."

And this statement right here pisses me off more than anything. I don't understand why he thinks he can treat me like shit when he starts drinking. Is it some kind of man code or something? I know some of the other guys don't act like this, but the sad fact is, most of them do.

I stare Jake down, and when he won't give an inch, I unleash. "Who the hell do you think you are? We've been dating for a long time, but that does not mean you can talk to me like I'm worthless. I'm leaving, and I don't care if I have to *walk* all the way home," I shout. "As far as I'm concerned, we are done. I'm tired of this shit, and can't take it anymore."

I notice everything has gone eerily quiet, and I glance around. Just fucking great. We've attracted a crowd. That was not my intention, but I can't deal with this anymore. It's the same thing every weekend, and I'm just tired of it. I love Jake, but not enough for this. Besides, we are going to different schools in the fall. I seriously doubt the long-distance thing would work anyway. Better to end it now, even if it is in front of the whole senior class. I love Jake, well, at least I did. Things have been strained between us lately. I don't feel connected to him the way I did before this last semester. We've started drifting. And now, we're just going through the motions. Staying together because we don't know how to be alone anymore. We shouldn't stay stagnant with each other, and I'm over being his pretty little lapdog.

I start walking to the driveway, and come to a halt when I hear him yelling behind me.

"That's okay bitch, keep walking. Now I don't have to deal with your moody ass anymore." He's laughing as he says all this.

I want to beat the hell out of him so bad. But I don't really want to cause any more of a scene. I already know that I'll be the talk of the town tomorrow, and I don't want to give them anything else to add to their gossip. I flip Jake the finger and continue on my merry way.

I should probably call my parents to come pick me up, but I'm a little buzzed and don't want to get a lecture. Walking is probably the dumbest idea I've had today. Well... besides telling Jake off in front of everyone. That ranks right up there at the top. I'm slowly making my way down the road when a car pulls up beside me.

"Do you need a lift?" a guy asks.

"No thanks," I say as I keep walking.

"You sure?"

I look in the car, and at the driver. He went to our school a couple of years ago. I don't remember his name, but he was always hanging around Cami's brother. I know this is probably a really bad idea, but I nod, open the door, and slide into the passenger seat. My feet are killing me, and I barely made it half a mile down the road. One day I'll learn not to wear heels to these events.

This dude looks completely sober. I know that I've seen him around, and I don't get any bad vibes off him, but I still keep my hand on the door handle just in case I need to jump out. Dramatic maybe, but I've seen those movies where girls getting in cars with strangers end up in a ditch somewhere.

"Rough night?" he asks.

"Yeah," I reply. "I'm not really in the mood to talk, but can you drop me off at my house? I'd really appreciate it."

He nods and we continue on in silence after I give him my address. It doesn't take long since we live in a pretty small town, and soon we're pulling into my parent's driveway.

I open the door, and hesitate. "Thanks for the ride."

"No problem. Glad I could make sure you got home safe," he says.

When I get out, I turn around and mystery guy gives me a quick wave. I wish I had asked him his name. Now I feel like a total bitch. But I'm also relieved to finally be home. I let myself in, slip off my shoes, and collapse on the couch. After that big showdown I don't even have the energy to go to my bed.

I check my phone, but there aren't any messages. I text

Cami letting her know that I'm home and that I'll text her in the morning. I'm sure she'll have questions after she finds out that I dumped Jake in front of everyone at the party.

I set my phone on the coffee table, grab the blanket that's thrown over the couch, and try my best to fall asleep.

* * *

There's pounding coming from the front door, and I jump up. What time is it? I look at my phone but it's dead since I forgot to put it on the charger last night. I stretch and then rush to the door to see who is knocking on the door like they're the police. I swing it open, and find Cami standing there, mid-knock.

"You look like hell," are the first words out of her mouth. "What happened to you last night? You just disappeared and then everyone was talking about how you dumped Jake for another guy, and all kinds of craziness!"

This is Cami at her finest. I love her to death, but she is way too dramatic. I grab her arm, yank her inside, and lead her to my room. I don't know why she even knocks. She has a key to our house. She practically lives here. We've been friends for what seems like forever, and she's the one I dump all my emotions on. And after last night, I need her.

As soon as we get into the room I blurt out, "What do you mean I dumped Jake for another guy?"

She shrugs like it isn't a big deal. "I don't know. That's just what he's telling everyone, and that you've been cheating on him the past couple of months. I know it's not true, but he's the one everyone is going to listen to."

"I can't believe that arrogant asshole! I mean, seriously. I've done nothing but whatever he wants to do since we've been together. How can I possibly be seeing someone else when I'm always with him?" I'm ranting I know, but come on.

Cami looks like she's about to start backing away from a feral animal. "I know, Tonya. Believe me, I know you would never do that. But that's what he's telling people. I just wanted to give you a heads up. Now enough with the idiotic ex-boyfriend talk. Let's grab some crap food and watch TV all day."

We walk out of the room and head to the kitchen. If there is one thing I specialize in its junk food. And it's just what I need right now to deal with this shit storm Jake is causing me. I wonder how bad the rumor has gotten since just last night. Cami knows because somehow, she's always the first to know everything. I just hope this doesn't get around to the entire town. I'll have to do some major damage control, and I don't really want my parents to hear whatever lies he thinks he needs to spread in order to keep his rep intact.

We fill our arms up with ice cream, cookies, popcorn and drinks. Cami must sense I'm not up to talking because she doesn't press me on my sudden silence. Instead, she grabs the blanket off the top of the couch and gets everything ready for us to start our *Vampire Diaries* marathon.

About halfway through the first season, Cami is sound asleep. I guess getting up at the ass crack of dawn after partying all night caught up with her. I make sure she is comfortable and hurry to my room. Grabbing my phone, I try to gather all the courage I can. Then I jab the speed dial icon, much harder than needed, and prepare to lay into this asshole who is now dead set on ruining my reputation.

Jake doesn't answer, of course. I don't know if he's still passed out from whatever hangover he has, or if he's avoiding my calls. This almost pisses me off worse than telling everyone I was cheating on him. If he's ignoring me that just shows how much of a coward he really is. He has no problem putting my name out there with lies, but the moment I try to call him on his bullshit, he's conveniently not available.

I'm beyond pissed at this point and I know nothing is going to calm me down but music at ear pounding levels. I grab my headset and pull up Bush's *Razorblade Suitcase* and try to let the sexy voice behind the angry lyrics bring me down. It's probably not the best choice of music to listen to right now, but I need something. I climb on my bed, close my eyes, and let my mind wander while Gavin's voice calms my nerves.

I'm not sure how much time passes but when I open my eyes my mom is standing over me. It scares the shit out of me, and I jump, almost hitting her in the face. It would be comical if she didn't have a stern look on her face.

"Tonya what in the world are you doing? And why is Cami asleep on the couch?" Mom starts badgering me. I glance at the clock and realize it's been a couple of hours. I'm actually surprised Cami is still here.

"Cami came over to get a sugar rush and fell asleep while watching TV. I came in here because I needed to blow off steam, and kind of zoned out. Why? You're looking at me like I've murdered someone." I know I probably don't want the answer to this question, but she looks awfully pale.

Mom sighs, "Baby girl, I've heard some... things. I'm sure they aren't true, but it's not something I like hearing around town. And it's even worse when one of my clients is gossiping to me about my own daughter. What happened last night?"

Now I'm fuming. It's one thing for my best friend to already have this ridiculous information, but for my mom to be hearing this crap pisses me off beyond belief. "What did you hear? Because I can tell you right now it's probably a bunch of bullshit."

Mom looks like she doesn't want to say what I already know is about to come out of her mouth. "Well, this person said that the quarterback's girlfriend has been screwing guys behind his back." She grimaces at how harsh she sounds. "And I told her that running her mouth probably isn't the best way to spend her time, and we would need to reschedule our appointment to a later time. Are you going to tell me what happened?"

Now it's my turn to sigh. I rub my temples as I fill Mom in on everything that happened last night.

I hate that pitying look Mom has on her face. But it quickly morphs into rage. It's pretty safe to say that I get my attitude and temperament from my mom. It doesn't take much to get us going, especially when it comes to family.

Mom bolts upright. "Are you kidding me! He's actually spreading those lies around town. After y'all have been together for so long. I know things have been a little rough with you two the past few months, but that doesn't mean he

215

has the right to give this town something to talk about. You deserve better than that, and did the right thing leaving his ass there." Her angry face is pretty terrifying right now. I don't think I've ever seen her so pissed.

I know my mom is itching to go hunt down the rat bastard, and make him sorry he ever wanted to be my boyfriend. I put a hand on her arm, and shake my head. "Mom, please let me handle this. I'm not some weakling who's afraid of confrontation. Jake will make this right. Gotta love living in Small Town, TX. Where rumors fly, and nobody listens."

Mom brings me in for a monster of a hug. "Go wake up Cami and meet me in the kitchen. This situation calls for brownies."

Mom sets out an array of cookies. I swear I don't know how she finds time to bake, work, and worry about me. She also pulls a carton of vanilla bean ice cream out of the freezer to top the warm gooeyness that are her cookies. There is no better way to eat them.

"This is the perfect way to get rid of boy problems," Mom says while pushing bowls of yummy goodness toward me and Cami. I nod in agreement. I can't think of a better way.

After stuffing our faces, Cami announces that she has to leave to have dinner with her dad. She comes from a seriously fucked up family. I don't understand how she is still even remotely sane.

I give her a hug, and thank her for letting me know about the shit storm that is headed my way.

I hear the front door open and then slam shut really

fast. I get up to see what's going on, and crash right into Cami.

"I thought—" I stammer out, but she quickly cuts me off.

"Tonya, you've got a problem," is all she says before she rushes out.

art assignment from reaf's point of view

THIS PROJECT IS GOING to be so easy. Thompson handed us the final exam of my dreams. It's a good thing, too. Working as much as I do to help my family doesn't give me much time to do homework. But if I'm going to make something of myself, I need to keep up with doing both.

Glancing up, I see the screen on one of the computers in the row ahead of me. My stomach plummets and my heart stops. No. I'm not going to let someone choose Picasso before me. It's not going to happen. Even if the girl looking the artist up, is the one I had a crush on at the beginning of the semester. The person I still have a crush on despite her growing belly and the possibility of her being with someone else.

The whole time we've been in the computer lab, I've been playing games because I already know who I want to do. I never thought I'd have to pick anyone else. Though, it should have crossed my mind because he is a popular, well-known artist.

The forty-five-minute research time is up, and I scoot

my chair back. The sound must have alerted her because she stands up so quickly I worry she's going to topple over. She walks toward Professor Thompson as if she's on a top-secret mission.

Shit, she beat me to him. More importantly, how does a pregnant woman move that fast? She's rambling about how she feels like she should be allowed to pick Picasso, even if he's well-known. A growl of frustration slips from my lips, and she rounds on me. Anger protruding from her stance. But she doesn't say anything, she only stares at me. That's it.

Ignoring her as best I can, I turn toward our professor. "Professor Thompson, I was going to pick Picasso."

"Now Reaf, Tonya here has already chosen Picasso. She got here first so you'll need to pick another artist."

Stuttering, I argue, "But... why can't we have two people do the same artist. Many of these works have vast differences, and different looks."

Professor Thompson considers this for a moment. "I guess I can bend the rules a little. Which piece are you wanting to reproduce?"

"Guernica." I don't hesitate. It's my favorite piece of art, and I've been itching to recreate it for a while.

Tonya eyes me, and it's starting to make me uncomfortable. Not because I'm intimidated by her, but because I want to know what she's thinking.

Thompson finally nods. "Okay, I'll put you down for that work." He writes something down in his notebook. "Since y'all have decided to do the same artist, I want a report from you that shows the diversity in an artist's portfolio...together."

We gape at him until we realize he's not going to change

his mind since neither of us are willing to give up the paintings we've requested. After a quick glance, Tonya grabs her things and hauls ass out of the computer lab. Is the thought of working with me that horrible? On the other hand, having to work with her on a project is going to take away work hours that I desperately need.

Rushing back to my chair, I grab my bag and hurry down the hall after her. I grab her arm, trying not to show my frustration at how many hours I'm going to lose. Apparently, I don't do a good job. Her eyebrows are scrunched together as she stares me down. Not giving a damn about what I have to say. "I guess since we're working together, I'll be seeing more of you."

I take her in from head to toe. She's beautiful, and whoever she's with is one lucky guy. Even if she has a crappy attitude sometimes. Without saying another word, I walk off. The only plus side in all of this is I'll get to know the girl I've been crushing on better.

acknowledgments

There are so many people to thank that I'm not even sure where to begin. To Vanessa, my soul sister, thank you for always being my cheerleader. I don't know how I would have gotten through this book without your constant motivation and words of encouragement. Stephanie, you have no idea how much you helped me finish this book. Your words of wisdom and telling me to sit my ass in the chair and write helped on more than once occasion. Tiffani, thank you for being my very first reader. You've cheered me on through all the changes this book has gone through. Tracy and Emily, thank y'all for being awesome friends and encouraging me. And Victoria, thank you for always answering my questions even though I felt pretty ridiculous asking what should be simple ones. And, thank you for helping me start this journey

Shelly at Small Edits, you are a rockstar at catching my errors and tightening up this book. Crystal at KP Designs, thank you for the awesome new covers.

To the Secret Sisterhood. Ladies, y'all make my days so much better. I'm beyond grateful for your support. Thank y'all for helping with all my questions.

To Mom and Dad: thank you for always supporting my dreams, and not rolling your eyes every time I begin a new endeavor. You taught me to chase my dreams while also keeping my feet planted firmly on the ground. Both of you let me stay up past bedtime to read when I should have been sleeping. Thank you for never taking away that flashlight I kept by my bed for late night reading. Your love and support mean everything to me.

My little family... I couldn't do this without you. There were nights with cereal for dinner and a messy house so that I could chase my dream. Hubs, Boy Child, and Wee One, this is for you.

And, finally, readers and bloggers. Thank you for taking a chance on my first book. Without you, this would be a file forgotten on my desktop.

also by katrina marie

The Taking Chances Series

Welcome to Your Life

Cruel & Beautiful World

Ways to Go

Remember That Night

My Only Wish is You

From This Moment

Shoot Down the Stars

Love will Save Your Soul

Take a Chance

Gone in Love Series

Gone Country

Gone Steady

Gone Again

Out of the Ashes Series

Cocktails & Crushes

Brews & Bartenders (Summer 2022)

Cocky Hero Club

Big Baller

Baseball & Broadway

about the author

Katrina Marie lives in the Dallas area with her husband, two children, and fur baby. She is a lover of all things geeky and Gryffindor for life. When she's not writing you can find her at her children's sporting events, or curled up reading a book.

You can find Katrina Marie online in the following places:
Sign up for my newsletter: https://www.subscribepage.com/KatrinaMarieNewsletter
Website: katrinamarieauthor.com

f facebook.com/katrinamarieauthor

twitter.com/katmarieauthor

instagram.com/katrinamarieauthor

BB bookbub.com/profile/katrina-marie

pinterest.com/katrinamarieauthor